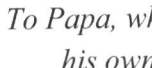
To Papa, wł
his own

MW01600557

1

Chapter 1

The automatic doors of the St. Augustine Emergency Room open, and a group of paramedics carefully hurry in with a stretcher. One of them approaches the front desk and says, "Car accident." The clerk looks at the pregnant woman lying on the stretcher and calls for a nurse. Nurse Abrams appears from the back and rushes over to the paramedics. She looks at the woman and asks, "Any injuries?" The lead paramedic shakes his head and answers, "Not that we can tell." The nurse looks at the woman again, this time analyzing every part of her body. Beads of sweat trickle slowly down the woman's cocoa colored face and settle at the top of her chest. Her moist eyes flutter as they attempt to avoid the bright ceiling lights bearing down on them from above. The rhythm of her quivering lips is matched by her twitching hands, both obvious indications of the agonizing pain coursing through her body. From these immediate observations, the seasoned nurse is able to discern the extent of the woman's condition. With her assessment complete, Nurse Abrams turns to the lead paramedic, and says, "We'll take it from here." She calls for help, and along with two male nurses, cautiously transfers the woman from the stretcher to an empty bed. Relieved of their duty, the paramedics thank the hospital staff, and return to the ambulance. The nurses carefully wheel the pregnant woman into one of the empty exam rooms and begin running tests on her. One of the male nurses suggests replacing the woman's clothes with a gown, but the proposal is shot down by Nurse Abrams.

Ten minutes later, the results from the tests come back, but none of them report anything troubling. The news is a relief to the three nurses, but their attention swiftly shifts to the next most pressing matter at hand. After a brief discussion, Nurse Abrams is picked to accompany the woman to the maternity ward, and as they prep her for transport, the nurse attempts to wake her up. She gently touches the woman's shoulder and whispers, "Ma'am?" The woman lets out a soft moan, but her eyes remain closed. The nurse tries again with a firmer grasp and a blunter tone. This time, it works, and the pregnant woman weakly opens her eyes.

She nervously scans the room and asks, "Where am I?" Nurse Abrams smiles and replies, "You're at the hospital. You were in an accident." The news shocks the woman, and she frantically remarks, "Is my baby…" Nurse Abrams touches her shoulder and says, "Your baby's fine. You didn't sustain any serious injuries. Do you remember where you were going before the crash?" The woman takes a deep breath and searches her memory for an answer. Watching the partially dazed woman struggle to recall the time before her accident worries Nurse Abrams, but she remains upbeat and patient.

By the time the woman is ready to respond, all of the transport preparations are complete, and a porter stands at the wait outside the room. The triggering event is a sharp pain in her abdomen, and like it, the woman's response is sudden and quick. "To the hospital; my water broke." The nurse springs into action and alerts the porter. The woman looks at the two of them and nervously asks, "What's happening? Where are you taking me?" Nurse Abrams touches the woman's left hand and says, "Don't worry ma'am. Everything's going to be alright. We're just going to move you upstairs so that you're more comfortable. Okay?" The woman nods and lets her head rest on the pillow beneath it. Nurse Abrams and the porter carefully guide the bed out of the exam room and towards the elevators. The two professionals move throughout the hospital with a graceful haste, but all the while, their demeanor remains calm. Even the woman's occasional groans and screams of pain are unable to shake their concentration. Upon reaching the elevators, Nurse Abrams looks at the woman, and asks, "How are you feeling ma'am?" She groans and weakly replies, "Back...hurts." The two words reveal more to the nurse than an entire book could, and in response, she mashes the top call button. Fortunately, a set of elevator doors open immediately, and the two professionals waste no time moving the bed into position.

After the elevator begins to move, Nurse Abrams takes a deep breath, and checks on her patient. Despite the cool temperature of the hospital, the woman's face is blanketed in sweat. Her breathing is rapid and desperate, but it's the only thing soothing her excruciating labor pains. However, the tears in her eyes betray her valiant efforts, and showcase how distinct and unimaginable the sensation she's experiencing is. The sight is a familiar one to Nurse Abrams, and no matter how many times she sees it, it unsettles her each and every time. The sound of the elevator doors opening redirects the nurse's focus, and she and the porter swiftly move the bed into the hall, where they're greeted by two nurses. Nurse Abrams relays the woman's condition to them, and they relieve her and the porter of their charge. The two nurses transport the woman to an empty birthing room, and after her bed is secured to the wall, they split up, with one alerting the doctor, and the other helping the woman change into a gown. Nurse Wallace finds Doctor McKaine coming out of the employee bathroom with a wet paper towel in his hands, and she informs him of the pregnant woman's arrival. He asks, "How many inches is she dilated", and Nurse Wallace answers, "We haven't checked yet, but based on her condition, at least five."

They hurry to the room and find the woman screaming in pain. Nurse Evans looks at the doctor and says, "She's dilated seven inches." Doctor McKaine nods and tells Nurse Wallace to begin preparations. She rushes out of the room, and down the right side of the hallway. Doctor McKaine approaches the left side of the bed, and asks, "Can you tell me your name?" The woman groans and weakly replies, "Alicia...Parker." The doctor smiles and says, "It's nice to meet you Ms. Parker. My name is Drew McKaine. I know you're feeling a little nervous, but rest assured, everything is going to be alright. Is there anyone you'd like us to call?" She shakes her head and mutters, "No." Another painful contraction occurs, and Ms. Parker squeezes Nurse Evan's hand. Despite the intense discomfort, for the pregnant woman's sake, she ignores the pain and continues to remain supportive. Doctor McKaine puts on a turquoise colored gown and washes his hands in a nearby sink. A few moments later, Nurse Wallace returns with the equipment in tow. She positions a stool in the room next to the bed and places the small tray of tools on top of it. The nurse puts on a face mask, and hands one to her fellow medic, who does the same.

Doctor McKaine sanitizes his hands for a third time before finally sheathing them with a pair of white gloves. He looks at the edge of the bed and says, "Nurse Wallace, can you please close the door?" The nurse nods and shuts the door to the room, separating it from the rest of the hospital. The relative isolation brings a sense of urgency to the situation. However, as with any battle, there is no turning back, and the only way forward is through. Nurse Evans sits beside Alicia Parker and acts as her emotional support, while Nurse Wallace assists the doctor with the delivery. To put Ms. Parker at ease, Doctor McKaine explains the procedure to her as he watches for signs of the baby. By the time he's finished, her cervix is fully dilated, and the time between contractions has slowed down considerably. The urge to push slowly overpowers the pain in Ms. Parker's lower body, and as the sensation reaches its climax, her baby's head makes its first appearance. Doctor McKaine positions his hands near her birth canal and instructs her to push. His tone, though considerate, is too soft for the aching woman's ears to hear, and as a consequence, the burden of coaxing and coaching Alicia Parker falls upon the two nurses. Seconds and minutes pass, but the baby remains lodged in its mother's body.

Although, the slow progress worries neither the doctor nor the nurses, and they valiantly continue to encourage Ms. Parker to keep pushing. Forty minutes later, the baby's head fully emerges, and lands in the doctor's hands. Doctor McKaine steadies his arms and focuses the whole of his energy on receiving the child safely and softly. Another three minutes pass before the rest of the baby is released, but the sight of the unraveling umbilical cord causes the doctor to smile. He carefully lifts the crying newborn and declares, "It's a boy." The two nurses smile, and Ms. Parker's face fills with tears. Doctor McKaine places the child on her chest, and the first thing she notices is the baby's heartbeat. In that moment, the enduring pain is overshadowed by an overwhelming feeling of joy. The newborn reaches out, and Ms. Parker takes hold of his tiny hand. In that moment, the nurses, the doctor, and the entire world all fade away, and the only thing that matters is the child lying on her chest. A name suddenly comes to Ms. Parker, and she whispers, "David." The baby responds with a soft cry, and his mother says, "Perfect."

Chapter 2

The moment of bliss is soon replaced by a haunting realization that lingers in Ms. Parker's mind even after she leaves the hospital. Alone and without any support, the new mother's concern shifts from the birth and health of her child to the near future and her ability to return to work. Were it up to her, the next three years would be entirely dedicated to nurturing her son and attending to his needs from sunrise to sunset. However, indulging that desire would not only lead to dire consequences, but it would also inevitably harm the child in the long run, unintentionally corrupting the young woman's good intentions. Thus, Ms. Parker's best option is to relish the time she can with her newborn son. Fortunately, six weeks are given to the young mother by her employer for that sole purpose. However, tied to this gracious policy are two heavy strings, reduced pay and a continuing obligation to a few job-related duties. Nonetheless, the terms are embraced wholeheartedly by Ms. Parker, and instead of aimlessly using the allotted time provided to hcr, shc trcats it with reverence and makes the absolute most of it. The young mother masterfully balances caring for her son and completing her daily tasks. Early mornings, late nights, and rude midnight awakenings all become a part of her ritual. Messy diaper changes, immense levels of fatigue, and short power naps become mundane occurrences. Yet, in the face of all these things, Ms. Parker's love for David spurns her forward, and never once does the young mother feel a hint of regret for bringing the boy into the world.

Strong is too weak a word to label her willpower and dedicated too passive a term to describe her conduct. In spite of this, the time passes by quickly, much to Ms. Parker's disappointment. Thinking ahead, the attentive mother had already prepared for her eventual return by enrolling her son in a local daycare. However, at the beginning of her partial leave, it felt like his first day was an eternity away. But on the Sunday before it, upon recalling the period of time, Ms. Parker realized how quickly it went. Monday morning brings a sense of relief, but also some regret as well. For a moment, she considers prolonging her return for a few more days, but the fleeting thought is immediately dominated by a more pragmatic one. The young mother gets out of bed and attends to her typical morning tasks, but her usual precise attitude is replaced by a conversely relaxed one.

Each moment Ms. Parker spends with her infant son is drawn out, and if not for her alarm clock, she would be late to work without even realizing it. The drive to the daycare is quiet except for a short conversation between the mother and one of its workers regarding her son's evening pick-up. Nestled between a physical therapy clinic and a small coffee shop, the unassuming red brick building was a welcome discovery to the young woman when she first learned she was pregnant. In the small town of Cartersville, Illinois, there were only two daycares to choose from.

Initially, Ms. Parker considered Rising Child Daycare as her first choice. Not only was the facility new, but it also received high praise from everyone she mentioned it to. A conversation with the manager reassured the young mother of her decision, and an in person visit to the facility was scheduled the same day. However, upon walking through the daycare's doors, the warm feeling Ms. Parker felt on the phone was replaced by a cold and awkward sensation. The reason for the sudden shift was not immediate to the mother, but after the short tour, it became fully apparent. Every room in the building was neat, organized, and pleasantly fragranced. But the caretakers, the manager, and even the majority of the children were of a single hue.

Blue and green eyes followed the young mother in and out of every room, as if waiting for her to do something sinister. Still, the day-care's amenities and well-rounded curriculum were alluring enough to cancel out her initial misgivings. But instead of making her decision that day, Ms. Parker chose to give it more thought at home. For three days, the choice was at the forefront of her mind, but she was no closer to a decision. And then, during a casual conversation with a neighbor, another daycare was nonchalantly mentioned. Ms. Parker reacted instantly and asked for more information about it.

The neighbor gave the daycare's name, Bright Hope Childcare, and a few miscellaneous details about the facility's history. But altogether, the overall description was lacking, and the young mother found herself determined to learn more about the newly discovered daycare. Thus, she spent the remainder of the day searching for any information available on Bright Hope, and after finally putting together a satisfying picture of the facility, she set up an in person visit for the next day. When Ms. Parker arrived at the building in the morning, her first thought was that she'd somehow misread the directions. However, the sight of the white and blue decal on the building's front door lifted that concern away.

Before heading inside though, the young mother took a moment to examine her surroundings. The area was far from unfamiliar; in fact, she passed by here almost every day. Yet, not once had she noticed the building, or considered it being a place for childcare. After a few more seconds of peeking around, Ms. Parker finally entered Bright Hope. A short young woman with curly black hair greeted her at the front desk, and said, "Hi, are you here for a pick-up?" The young mother answered, "No, I'm here for a visit."

A smile brighter than a thousand suns appeared on the young woman's face, and she giddily remarked, "You must be Ms. Parker! My name's Hazel. I spoke to you on the phone yesterday. It's so nice to meet you." Her pleasant presence caught the young mother off guard, but at the same time, it filled her heart with a warm feeling. She smiled without even realizing it, and replied, "It's nice to meet you as well. I hope I'm not too early. I know our appointment isn't till eleven." Hazel shook her head and happily remarked, "Of course you're not too early. You're welcome to come any time you like. I was just about to check on the kids anyway." The young woman led Ms. Parker into the back of the building, and showed her the classrooms, the nursery, and even the bathrooms. Throughout the short journey, the two of them ran into both children and caretakers, and each time, they were greeted with smiles and waves.

Not once did Ms. Parker feel uncomfortable or awkward, and after returning to the lobby, she felt ready to make her decision. Her only concern was the building's age, which was easily noticed during the tour. Unlike Rising Child, most of the furnishings, while in good condition, were almost as old as Ms. Parker herself. The presented curriculum was slightly less extensive than the other daycare's as well, but in spite of these things, there was little doubt about which of the two she would choose.

And standing in front of the building on the fateful first day, no regret enters her heart. With David secured in her arms, Ms. Parker carefully heads into the daycare. Alice, one of the facility's other caretakers, greets the mother and son in the lobby, and says, "It's so good to see you again." She places a sign in sheet and pen in front of the young mother, and asks, "Has David's schedule changed at all?" Ms. Parker fills in one of the blank rows on the sheet and replies, "No, it's the same." After she places the pen down, Alice walks around the desk, and says, "We'll take good care of him." The smile on her face eases some of the young mother's worry, but the uneasy feeling persists as she gives David to the caretaker.

Seeing her child in another person's arms sends an unnerving chill through her spine, and in an attempt to suppress the troublesome feeling, she forces herself to smile. The expression appears cracked, however, and the sentiment buried beneath is instantly picked up by Alice's keen eye. To put the nervous mother at ease, the caretaker approaches her, and says, "Say goodbye to mommy." David smiles and gleefully reaches out to his mother. Ms. Parker responds to her baby's call by letting him touch her face.

The child's soft touch soothes her worried soul, and though still reluctantly, she leaves after planting a kiss on David's cheek. The baby reacts to his departing mother with a yearning cry, but Ms. Parker remains steadfast, and continues walking until she's back in her car. During her drive to work, her mind bounces between it and the daycare, but the former takes center stage once she reaches her desk. The young mother's first day back consists of catching up, completing newly assigned tasks, and accepting congratulations from coworkers. Time passes at a normal pace, but when five o'clock arrives, her focus shifts entirely to picking up David.

Though Ms. Parker assumes a composed demeanor on the way to the daycare, her conduct conveys an attitude that is entirely different. The speed at which she drives is quicker than usual, and her pace after arriving is similarly hasty. The young mother is met in the lobby by Alice, and after she fills in the sign out sheet, the caretaker goes into the back of the building to retrieve David. A few minutes later, she appears from the hallway with the infant in her arms. The sight of the baby's happy face makes Ms. Parker smile, and as Alice gives him to her, she asks, "How did he do?"

The caretaker sighs and replies, "He was a little upset at first, but he was quiet for most of the day. We were a little worried when we didn't hear him crying for a while." The young mother looks at the infant, and remarks, "That's good to hear. What activities did he do today?" Alice crosses her arms and replies, "He did some crawling practice, and we read a few picture books. He seems to really like them. One of the only times he cried was after I finished reading." The news makes Ms. Parker delighted, and she jubilantly remarks, "That's great!" After a couple more minutes of conversation with the caretaker, the young mother departs the daycare with her son in tow. On the way home, she stops at the store, and picks up a few picture books. Once in the house, Ms. Parker places David in his crib, and allows herself an hour to unwind.

She spends the rest of the day feeding, cleaning, and enjoying the free time with her son. At seven o'clock, she gives the infant a bath, and puts him to bed. Exhausted both physically and mentally, the only thing on the young mother's mind as she lies on her bed is the next day. At ten o'clock, she meanders through her nightly routine, and settles into her own bed. However, as with most nights, her motherly duties extend well into the midnight hour, and by the time she's given an undisturbed period of sleep, the first signs of morning are present.

The next day goes by similarly, with only a few minor differences sprinkled throughout it. It takes Ms. Parker two weeks to adapt to her new routine, and even longer to adjust to the sleep deprivation associated with it. But over time, dropping her son off in the morning and picking him up in the evening become mundane. On the other hand, watching him grow up is absolutely exciting to the young mother, and each day brings something new. At five and a half months, David utters his first word, and by nine, the baby boy is able to repeat five more. With every passing day, more of the world is revealed to the child, and Ms. Parker documents each discovery with a photograph. Nurtured by his mother and teachers, the young boy matures like a carefully tended plant. Shapes, colors, and the alphabet, once completely foreign concepts, become recognizable and simple. Picture books are replaced by chapter books and blocks are replaced by action figures. Daycare becomes preschool. Preschool becomes kindergarten. And finally, after six years of pitfalls and triumphs, the young boy enters a new stage of his life, one that will unknowingly set the tone for the rest of it.

Chapter 3

The sight of her son makes Ms. Parker smile. The young boy stands ready at the door, with a book bag strapped to his back and an eager expression on his face. From shirt to shoes, every part of his outfit is brand new. In celebration of the young boy's first day of elementary school, the previous day was mostly spent preparing for it. After a haircut in the morning, the bulk of the afternoon consisted of shopping for clothes, groceries, and school supplies. The evening was used by the mother and son to play board games and watch a movie. At eight o'clock, the young boy bathed, set his clothes out, and went to sleep excited and ready for the next day. No alarm was needed the following morning; both mother and son were up early. Young David finished his morning routine in record time, and even beat his mother to the door. Ms. Parker grabs her purse from a chair beside the front closet and asks, "Are you ready?" David nods and joyfully exclaims, "Yes!" The mother and son head out of the house, and the young boy runs to the car. Ms. Parker unlocks it, but remarks, "Be careful." David replies, "Sorry", and jumps into the back seat of the gray sedan. The boy's excitement makes his mother pick up her own pace, and she hurries to the driver's seat after locking the front door. The smile remains on David's face during the drive to the school. Although only fifteen minutes pass before the front entrance of Cartersville Elementary School comes into view.

A sea of parents and children stands in front of the large orange brick building. Teachers and staff cautiously weave through the crowd, guiding and organizing it like a shepherd would a flock of sheep. With the staff's guidance, the scattered mass slowly turns into twenty-five crooked lines. David watches the scene unfold in awe, and eagerly wishes to join the fray as well. Sensing her son's impatience, Ms. Parker searches the street for a parking spot. She finds one a block down from the school, in front of a small park. As soon as the car comes to a complete stop, David springs from the back seat, and runs onto the sidewalk. But before the overjoyed boy can go any further, his mother says, "Wait for me." The gravity in her voice makes the six year old stop right away, and his ecstatic attitude quickly mellows. After locking the car, Ms. Parker meets her son on the sidewalk, and the two of them walk towards the school hand in hand. As they get closer to the building, the young boy's grip gets tighter, and his pace increases. Ms. Parker matches her son's tempo each time, but her focus is primarily on the school's lawn. In the time it took for the mother to park her car, the amount of people in front of the school significantly decreased. The majority of the parents are either gone or leaving, while the students sit in small lines with teachers at the heads of them.

Ms. Parker scans the area and asks, "Do you remember who your teacher is?" David smiles and replies, "Mrs. Myriam." Ms. Parker looks at the lawn again, and sees a teacher holding a poster with that written on it. She waves at the woman and says, "I think that's her." David notices the sign and excitedly waves as well. The teacher returns the friendly gesture and beckons the mother and son to her. Ms. Parker and David cross the wide concrete pathway, and walk onto the grass. They follow the line up to the front, and when they reach Mrs. Myriam, she outstretches her hand and jubilantly says, "Hi." Ms. Parker shakes the teacher's hand and replies, "Hello, my name is Alicia Parker." Mrs.

Myriam smiles and remarks, "It's nice to meet you Ms. Parker. I'm Mrs. Myriam." The teacher turns her attention to the child standing beside the mother, and asks, "What's your name?" The young boy shyly replies, "David", and Mrs. Myriam smiles and says, "It's nice to meet you as well David. Are you ready to learn a lot this year?" The young child's excitement returns, and he swiftly nods his head. His enthusiasm puts a smile on his mother's face and the teacher's, and the latter remarks, "That's good to hear. Why don't you find a spot in line and introduce yourself to some of your classmates."

David looks at his mother, and she gives him a nod of approval. The young child hurries to the back of the line and sits behind a girl with a blue book bag. With her son situated, Ms. Parker thanks Ms. Myriam, and heads back to her car. As she passes by David, she says, "I'll see you this evening." He waves and replies, "Okay." The young boy continues waving at his mother until she's out of sight. Being alone draws much of the fervor out of the child, and as a consequence, his excited demeanor calms. However, remembering his teacher's words, David's attention shifts to a new activity. He lightly touches the right shoulder of the girl with the blue book bag, and she turns around and silently looks at him. The young boy smiles and says, "Hi, my name is David", but without uttering a single word, the girl turns back around. The rejection confuses David, and an awkward feeling blankets him. The young boy searches his body for anything out of the ordinary, but he's unable to find a single thing. For the briefest moment, he considers attempting to ask the girl why she didn't respond, but the idea is shattered by fear of another rejection. Instead, David decides to quietly wait and listen for Mrs. Myriam's next instructions. Fortunately, he doesn't have to wait long. After the last of the new students trickle in, the teacher lowers her poster, and says, "Okay everybody, we're going to go inside now. Are you all ready?"

The children in Mrs. Myriam's line spring to their feet and loudly reply, "Yes." She turns to the school and remarks, "Make sure you stay in line so you don't get lost." The teacher leads her class into the school, and down the left side of the main hallway. The interior of the building is a welcoming and stunning sight to the students. The ceiling lights illuminate the baby blue walls and polished ceramic floor, and colorful signs and stickers decorate every door. One sign in particular catches David's eye, and as he passes by it, he whispers, "You can be and do anything." Mrs. Myriam stops at a door on the left side of the hallway, and says, "Okay everyone, we're here." She opens it, and the students quietly file in one by one. After all of them are inside the classroom, Mrs. Myriam shuts the door, and tells her students to stand by the wall.

The children huddle in the right corner of the room and wait for their teacher's next directions. Mrs. Myriam walks to the front of the class and grabs a dry erase marker from a tray underneath the white board. She looks at her students and says, "Each desk has a nametag on it. Find the one with your name and introduce yourself to the rest of your desk buddies." The children spread throughout the classroom and search the five desk clusters for their names. David finds his at the cluster closest to the reading area.

He sits and places his backpack next to his chair, and after another minute, a blonde-haired boy joins him, and says, "Hi." David opens his mouth, but stops himself before any words can come out. The other boy is undeterred by his hesitation though, and happily remarks, "My name's Alex." His friendly demeanor wipes away the reluctance in David's heart, and he smiles and replies, "I'm David." With the ice sufficiently broken between the two boys, they become lost in conversation, and even after being joined by two additional students, their dialogue only grows. After ten more minutes, Mrs. Myriam finally calls for her student's attention.

It takes a few seconds for the children to quiet down, but as soon as they do, she begins talking. "I hope you all introduced yourselves to your desk mates. They're going to be the people you spend the most time with this year. But before we talk about that, let's go around the room and introduce ourselves to one another."

She looks at the group of desks closest to her and remarks, "We'll start here and go from right to left." The four students look at each other, but none of them volunteers to go first. Their innocent shyness puts a smile on Mrs. Myriam's face, and to encourage her students, she says, "I'll go first as an example. I'm Mrs. Myriam. I've lived in Cartersville my entire life. My favorite color is purple, and I wanted to be a teacher ever since I was a little girl."

Her honest and cheerful tone soothes many of the students' timidness, and one of the girls in the front group stands and says, "Hi, my name is Annabelle, and my favorite color is green." After she sits, the boy beside her stands, and gives a similar introduction. It takes a few minutes for the first group to finish introducing themselves, but by then, the rest of the children eagerly await their turn to talk. One by one, each boy and girl gives information about themselves. Some are concise and straightforward, while others are liberal and carefree, and a few of the introductions garner laughter.

The closer David's turn gets, the more excited he becomes, and when his group's opportunity to speak arrives, he shoots out of his chair before any of the other students can. "My name is David, and my favorite color is yellow. I like to read and write for fun. When I get older, I want to write stories for everyone." Satisfied with his statement, the young boy goes to sit down, but before his back touches the seat, Mrs. Myriam remarks, "What about sports? You don't want to play any sports when you get older?" The question catches David by surprise, and unsure how to answer it, he nervously looks around the room. The young boy's uneasy feeling is compounded by his classmate's stares, and in an effort to free himself from the awkward predicament, he replies, "I don't really...watch sports."

A look of genuine shock appears on Mrs. Myriam's face, but she swiftly regains her composure, and remarks, "Oh, well that's okay. Writing books is good too." Relieved at last, David swiftly sits, and one of the girls in his group stands next. The rest of the introductions go by without issue, and after the last student speaks, Mrs. Myriam shifts to another topic. For the remainder of the morning, she details the rest of the day's activities, and runs through the daily schedule with her students.

At noon, she has the students line up, and guides them to the lunchroom. As they enter the other side of the school, David soaks in every new detail in sight, noting the different posters, banners, and rooms they pass by. Following their arrival, they're joined by three other classes, and the teachers show their students where to grab their trays and how to get their food. At first, the process appears daunting to the young boy, but his fears are swiftly put to rest by the kind workers. After receiving his food, David sits next to Alex and the rest of his class at the middle table. The two boys spend lunch eating and talking about their favorite books, and when the period ends, Mrs. Myriam has her class line up once more.

On the way back to the classroom, she stops at the bathrooms, and divides the students between them. The boys enter in groups of four and the girls in groups of threes. David's turn comes after the second group is finished. He and three other boys shuffle through the tall wooden door, and into the bland cream-colored room. David chooses the farthest urinal, and the other boys file into the remaining three. None of them say anything while they relieve themselves, but after David finishes, he suddenly notices something strange. Out of the corner of his right eye, the young boy spots three pairs of blue eyes looking in his direction.

Instinctively, he turns to meet the other boys' gazes, but their heads are pointed forward by the time his eyes reach them. Yet, nothing is said, not even by David himself. Instead, he ignores the occurrence, and goes to one of the sinks. He watches the other sink while washing his hands, but the boy at it doesn't look his way. In fact, none of the three boys looks at David the rest of the time they're in the bathroom. He leaves first, followed shortly thereafter by the other boys, and rejoins the line. As the next group enters the bathroom, David turns to Alex, and asks. "Did anyone look at you while you were peeing?" The other boy shakes his head and replies, "No. Why would they?"

The question rattles around in the young boy's mind for a minute, but he can't find an answer, and rather than giving one, he decides to change the subject. It takes fifteen additional minutes for the rest of the students to finish using the bathroom, and another five to complete the journey to the classroom. As they re-enter the room, Mrs. Myriam instructs her students to sit in the reading area, and the children hurry over to the large multicolored carpet. David sits in the middle, and Alex sits beside him.

Once all of the students are seated, Mrs. Myriam grabs three books from the small shelf beside the carpet, and says, "Okay kids, now we're going to do a little bit of reading, and you're going to pick which book we start with. When I say the title of each one, raise your hand if you want me to read it first. But remember, you can only raise your hand for one book. Does everyone understand?" The students nod, and Mrs. Myriam presents the first book. Its cover is a mix of orange, red, and yellow, and below the title is a similarly colored animal juggling a ball. Mrs. Myriam lets her students look at the book for a minute, and then moves on to the next one. The cover of the second book is much more simplistic. Its background is a subtle baby blue, and underneath the boldface title is a young dark-skinned girl with curly black hair.

As with the first book, Mrs. Myriam lets the children look at the cover for a brief period of time before moving on. However, the amount of time she spends on the second book is shorter than that of the first. After the allotted time passes, Mrs. Myriam returns the second book to her lap and presents the final one. Of the three, the third book is the least colorful. The entire cover, including the title, is colored with white and black stripes, and fittingly, the character pictured on it is a zebra. Mrs. Myriam lets the children look at the book for two minutes, and then remarks, "All right, now that you've seen each one, let's pick which one we're going to read. Remember, you can only raise your hand once; so, choose carefully."

She picks up the first book, and on cue, hands shoot into the air. Mrs. Myriam counts them and giddily remarks, "It might be close." She puts down the first book and raises the second one, but only two hands enter the air. Mrs. Myriam and the other students look at David and Alex, but neither party says anything. The sight makes the teacher feel somewhat sympathetic, and instead of moving on to the next book right away, she waits for a few more seconds. But none of the other children join the two boys, and as soon as Mrs. Myriam presents the third book, Alex and David's hands fall to the floor. They're replaced by those of the remaining students', which the teacher counts, and says, "It looks like this one's the winner."

She puts the other books away and begins reading. Though the book is short and mostly full of pictures, Mrs. Myriam engages her students by asking questions throughout it, and despite not being the book of his choice, David is attentive regardless. His hand is always the first in the air, and when given the opportunity to answer, he does so with confidence and sincerity. In an attempt to give the timid students a chance to speak, Mrs. Myriam politely asks the extroverted ones to take a break from answering questions.

Though the teacher's request is general, its primary target is obvious. Yet, rather than shame, Mrs. Myriam's statement causes David to smile, and his pride to swell. Nevertheless, the young boy obeys his teacher's request, and withdraws from the activity. After running out of questions, Mrs. Myriam puts the book away, and has the students return to their seats. The children spend the rest of the day coloring and conversing with each other. A light bell from the intercom signals the end of class, and a wave of excitement washes over the students. They grab their bags, line up at the door, and Mrs. Myriam walks them to the front of the school.

Once they're outside, the children quickly disperse, and go to their parents. David does the same, and runs to the sidewalk, where his mother waits. He greets her with a smile and a hug, and as he breaks away from Ms. Parker, she asks, "How was your day?" The young boy cheerily replies, "Good", and the two of them talk about their days on the way to the car. However, after putting on his seatbelt, David suddenly asks, "Mommy, is something wrong with me?" The question shocks Ms. Parker, but she hastily replies, "No, of course not." She looks at her son, but the child's face is blank and emotionless, as if the happiness has been completely drained from it. "Why would you think that", she asks.

David lowers his head and replies, "I said hi to this girl in our line, but she didn't say anything back." Hearing the sorrow in her son's voice hurts Ms. Parker's heart, and she asks, "Were you polite?" David nods, but remorsefully remarks, "Maybe I shouldn't have touched her shoulder." An unnerving thought creeps to the surface of the mother's mind, but she suppresses it with a cynical doubt, and says, "Next time, let her talk to you first. She may have just been nervous. You have to remember, not everyone is as outgoing as you are." David absorbs his mother's advice like a dry sponge in a bucket of water. "I'm sorry." Ms. Parker smiles at her son and remarks, "It's okay. You're still learning."

She starts the car, but before entering the street, she suddenly takes her hands away from the wheel. Unwilling to remain silenced, the unsettling thought forces its way back to the forefront of the mother's mind, and like an unbearably strong itch, it refuses to be left unscratched. "What did the girl look like?" The question catches David off guard, but he candidly answers, "She had blonde hair and blue eyes." The young boy's innocent response makes Ms. Parker smile, but the expression quickly disappears. Though incomplete, the description is more than enough for the mother, and a familiar feeling of dread grips her heart.

The sudden shift in her demeanor is noticed by David, and curious, he asks, "Why?" Ms. Parker takes a deep breath and answers, "Just wondered." The child accepts the response, but the mother doesn't. She feels guilty for intentionally withholding her true thoughts from her son. At the same time though, his acceptance of her answer brings relief and postponement of the need to expose a depressing reality to her son. The majority of the drive home goes by quietly, but as Ms. Parker parks in front of their house, David abruptly asks, "Is it bad that I don't like sports?"

Again, the question surprises his mother, but without hesitation, she compassionately replies,

"No. Did someone tell you it was?" The young boy shakes his head and timidly replies, "No." Ms. Parker can tell her son is lying, but she decides not to question him any further. Instead, the mother reconsiders her previous stance, and its justification. Knowing her son all too well, revealing the true nature of the situation with the young girl would undoubtedly taint his innocent outlook on the world. The joyful boy would never be the same way again, and every encounter would be met with an instinctive and burdensome caution. Yet, allowing her son to remain ignorant and rose colored would only cause irreparable harm later in life when the carefully crafted facade is finally cracked. The decision is a bitter one, but understood by Ms. Parker as necessary, and as she and her son walk into the house, her mind is consumed by how to tell her beloved child the world hates him, and why nothing he ever does will change that.

Chapter 4

Ms. Parker looks at the report card and takes a sip of coffee. She scans the white piece of paper, analyzing each letter grade and teacher's comment. Her eyes settle on David's Mathematics grade and the short comment beside it. Ms. Parker lets out a long sigh and loudly asks, "Are you ready to go?" David hurries downstairs and replies, "Yes, I'm ready." As he enters the kitchen, Ms. Parker stands, and asks, "Why do you have a C in Math?" The young boy looks at the floor and reluctantly replies, "I'm not good at taking tests." Ms. Parker picks up the report card and remarks, "Your teacher says you aren't paying attention in class." She walks past her son and into the front room. David senses the disappointment in his mother's voice, and a feeling of guilt briefly overwhelms him. He follows behind her and says, "I'll do better. I promise." Ms. Parker acknowledges the sincerity in her son's tone, but memories of previous statements similar to it taints her ability to believe it. She hands the report card to him and remarks, "Until it improves, no TV or video games. C's aren't going to cut it in high school, and you've only got three years left till then." The punishment frustrates the young boy, and without thinking, he angrily says, "But the rest of my grades are fine!" However, his mother's fierce reaction to the outburst drains all of the fervor out of him and replaces it with a timid remorse. Ms. Parker takes a deep breath and bluntly remarks, "You can do better, much better." Yet, despite her steadfast and immovable demeanor, she still feels a touch of uncertainty regarding her decision.

In truth, other than David's grade in Math, the rest of them are perfect, and concerning the less than satisfactory mark, even she knows there's plenty of time for him to improve it. However, Ms. Parker's own experiences with failure motivate her to do everything in her power to keep her son from slipping into mediocrity, and thus, she sees the situation as infinitely more dire than it truly is. Though to the young boy, the punishment is simply an unfair overreaction, and in an attempt to explain her reasoning, the mother condenses the feelings within her and says, "I'm only saying something because I care." David looks at the wall and mutters, "Okay." He trudges up the stairs and into his room. Ms. Parker thinks of saying something else, but a sudden noise from her pants pocket steals her attention. She looks at her phone and the notification on its screen. 'Time for work', it reads. The alert sends the mother into a panic, and she hastily retrieves her keys and purse from her room. As she hurries back downstairs, she announces, "I'm leaving, David." But before Ms. Parker can leave, her son appears at the top of the stairs, and asks, "Can you give me a ride to school."

She turns to him and remarks, "I'm running late today. Is something wrong with the bus?" David looks away and replies, "No, it's just…" The young boy doesn't finish though, and instead quietly returns to his bedroom. Ms. Parker sighs and says, "Maybe tomorrow. I love you." David murmurs a response, but his mother is out of the house before she can hear it. The young boy looks at the alarm clock on his nightstand and lazily rolls off his bed. He grabs his keys and phone from his dresser, and his book bag from the floor. He briefly looks over his room to make sure he has everything, and once assured, he turns off the lights and leaves the house. A gentle breeze greets David on the porch, and after locking the front door, he walks down the stairs and onto the sidewalk. As the young boy walks to his bus stop, he watches the clouds, and when the sun comes into view, a smile appears on his face. But after reaching his destination, the serene feeling is replaced by a dread.

The yellow school bus pulls in front of David, and for a moment, he considers turning around and going home. The idea fades away though once the bus's doors open, and the smile on his face disappears along with it. David boards the bus, and as he enters the aisle, the driver impatiently closes the door. The bus suddenly jerks forward, and the young boy has to hold onto the top of the two front seats to keep from falling down. Fortunately, the near pratfall goes largely unnoticed.

However, as he walks down the aisle, the other students stare and murmur amongst themselves. David keeps his gaze forward though, refusing to acknowledge any of their whispers, and finds an empty seat near the back of the bus. He carefully sits beside the window, places his book bag next to himself, and grabs a large red and white book out of its side pouch. As he opens it, the bus stops again, and picks up another student. The new arrival's presence sends the other students into a frenzy, and their combined noise becomes too much for the young boy to ignore. Unable to enjoy his book, David unzips his bag, but another boy sits next to him before he can put it away. He tries to move his book bag, but the other boy grabs it, and says, "Yo Dave, what's good man?"

Many of the nearby students look over their seats and curiously watch the scene unfold. One girl laughs and remarks, "Leave him alone Zach. He don't like us." The boy puts his arm around David and remarks, "Nah, we cool. He just a little shy." The gesture makes David uncomfortable, and he attempts to break free of the other boy's grasp, but Zach refuses to let him go. The sight of his peer squirming makes him smile, and only after getting bored does he finally let go. David doesn't say a single word, however, and quickly puts his book bag in between his feet.

Zach is unfazed by the reaction though, and scoots closer to him. He laughs and asks, "Why you don't talk to us?" David remains silent and turns to the window, but the other boy continues to pester him. "You think you better than us cuz you speak proper? Why you wanna be white so bad?" The spectating students react to the question with laughter, and Zach eagerly soaks up their attention. Still, David doesn't respond, and sensing the ineffectiveness of his taunting, Zach turns his attention to the book beside him. He picks it up and asks, "What's this?" Initially, David is unconcerned by the question, but when he realizes what the other boy is referring to, his demeanor completely changes.

Without hesitation, he reaches for the book, and tries to snatch it from Zach's hands. Unfortunately, the other boy reacts quicker, and pulls the book away before David's hand can get near it. The frustrated expression on his face is amusing to Zach, and the laughter coming from the rest of the students only makes the feeling better. But it isn't enough to satisfy him, and the desire for more of his peers' approval motivates him to go even farther. Thus, instead of returning the book, he carelessly tosses it across the aisle. A boy in a blue shirt catches it and announces, "I got it!"

The other boys react by calling for it next, while the girls watch them and laugh. The boy in the blue shirt tosses the book towards the back of the bus, and a boy with a black jacket snags it out of the air. In the process, the front cover is bent and nearly ripped. But the damage is ignored, and in no time at all, the book is in the air once again. David helplessly watches in horror as the other boys toss his book back and forth across the aisle. As it returns to Zach for the third time, David lunges at him in a final attempt to get it back, but the other boy pushes him away. He tries again, but Zach pushes him away again. Fueled by irritation and willpower, the young boy tries over and over to retrieve his book, but he's repulsed each time. After the seventh attempt, David's patience finally breaks, and instead of going for the book again, he throws a wild punch.

His fist strikes Zach's left cheek, and nearly causes him to fall off the seat. The act catches all of the onlooking students completely by surprise, and the reactions are numerous. Some gasp, others smirk, and a few are too shocked to say or do anything. However, the most stunned by the incident are Zach and David. The former is too shaken up to even think, and the stinging sensation in his cheek is the only thing he can focus on. The latter, thoroughly depleted of his rage, is filled wholly with regret.

As David's hand falls to his side, one of the students suddenly yells, "He punched Zach!" The remark snaps Zach out of his daze, and his shock is replaced by fury. He curls his right hand into a fist and slowly approaches David from the edge of the seat. With nowhere to run, the frightened and helpless young boy desperately raises his arms and waits for his beating. Seeing the terror on David's face makes Zach relish his inability to escape and the opportunity to punish him even more. But as he prepares to deliver his first strike, the bus suddenly stops, and the driver yells, "Leave him alone!" All of the students look forward, and Zach backs away from David right away. The driver puts the bus in park and says, "Give him back his book, and move to another seat."

The majority of the students return to their seats, but Zach continues to firmly stare at the front of the bus. Undeterred by the child's insolence, the driver takes his hands off the wheel, and bluntly remarks, "We're not leaving this spot till you give the book back and move." Zach glares at David, but obeys the driver's command. He returns the book and moves to a seat a few rows behind him. Still, the driver doesn't change the gear until Zach touches the back of his seat. The remainder of the ride goes by in silence, and when they reach the school, the students file out of the bus similarly quietly.

As Zach passes by the driver, he glares at him, but the older man is completely unfazed. After he exits the bus, the driver looks into the rearview mirror, and asks, "Are you coming?" David stands up and shuffles down the aisle, but before stepping off the bus, he turns to the driver and says, "Thank you." The older man nods and replies, "Sure thing." The young boy is absorbed by the sea of students as soon as he touches the sidewalk, and if not for his height, he wouldn't know where he was going. Even worse, the lack of space causes the students to awkwardly bump against one another as they walk toward the school's entrance. For David, the discomfort of the situation is magnified by the fact that most of the people nearby him are girls, one of whom he has a crush on.

Fortunately, the embarrassing situation ends inside the building, and after being freed from the mass, David heads to his locker. He checks his phone along the way, and each passing minute makes him move faster. The young boy wastes little time at his locker, only stopping to grab his Social Studies book. As he relocks it, he feels something touch his book bag, and turns around. A boy with long brown hair walks by and says, "Hey." The student is unfamiliar, but David waves at him anyway, and replies, "Hi."

The encounter puts a smile on the young boy's face that persists throughout his journey to homeroom. Although, after walking through the class's door, David realizes something strange. From the time between leaving his locker and reaching his homeroom class, each student he passed by either snickered or laughed. At first, he chalked the occurrence up to unfounded paranoia, but after it continued despite multiple hallway changes, it began to worry him. However, the investigation is interrupted by his teacher, who says, "David?" He turns to her and replies, "Yes, Mrs. Mathers?" She stands and quietly asks, "Can you come over here for a second?" The request confuses and somewhat scares the young boy, but he nevertheless walks over to his teacher's desk. "Did I do something wrong", he asks. Mrs. Mathers smiles and replies, "No, of course not. Can you turn around for me."

David remarks, "Okay", and obediently turns around. The teacher plucks a taped piece of paper from the back of the young boy's book bag, and reads the message scrawled across it. The smile disappears from her face in an instant, and she says, "You can turn back around now." David faces her and notices the piece of paper in her hands. "What's that", he asks. The clueless expression on the boy's face makes the teacher's heart sink to the floor, and she struggles to maintain her composure while looking at him. However, his curiosity, spurned even more by cluelessness, is unavoidable, and though hesitantly, she hands him the piece of paper. David looks at it and mumbles, "Oh."

He reads the word over and over, and each time, it feels as if a dagger is being pushed further into his heart. His face remains emotionless though, as if unsurprised by the situation altogether. He hands the piece of paper back to Mrs. Mathers, and she asks, "Do you know who put it there?" The young boy shakes his head and replies, "No." All of a sudden, the bell rings, and students flood into the class. David looks at his teacher and remarks, "Thank you." Mrs. Mathers crumples the piece of paper and attempts to respond, but the boy is already gone before she can get out a single word. For a couple minutes, she watches him locate a desk in the back of the room, but her attention is drawn away by the other students.

The chaos of the morning consumes the teacher's time without her realizing it, and by the time she's allowed a free minute, the bell has already rung. In response to the familiar sound, the students grab their bags, and hurry out of the class. From her desk, Mrs. Mathers observes David as he walks to the door. Despite the amount of time that has passed, his expression is the same as it was after seeing the note attached to his book bag. The young boy uses the facade of emotionlessness as a mask to cover his true feelings, but like a crack across an egg, his eyes reveal the truth underneath.

The guise is easily seen through by Mrs. Mathers, and an unsettling feeling of regret washes over the teacher as soon as David walks through the doorway. Yet at the same time, the thought of the boy's sorrow filled eyes is clouded by uncertainty regarding how to act, and the presence of her first class forces Mrs. Mathers to tuck the unpleasant feelings away. David's focus, on the other hand, is split between the morning's incident and the rest of the school day. His concern regarding the former is tied to fear, and the sentiment is only strengthened by the passing glances of his peers.

If not for his unknowing participation in the prank, it would barely register as an issue for him, and by the end of the day it may be forgotten altogether. Its potential reach paired with his oblivious demeanor, unfortunately, creates an anxiety within the boy that is not easily shaken. In spite of this, his outlook on the remainder of the day remains hopeful, and his goal continues to be salvaging it as much as possible. As he walks through the doorway of his Social Studies class, he waves at his teacher, and says, "Good morning." Ms. Patterson smiles and replies, "Good morning David. How are you doing?" He sighs and responds, "I'm doing okay."

Being one of the first students in the class, David has an abundance of choices regarding where to sit. The two front rows are empty, but he chooses a desk closest to the back wall. As he sits, Ms. Patterson asks, "Are you sure you can see from that far away?" David places his bag beside his desk and replies, "Yes, I can see." His teacher is somewhat skeptical of the response, but he proves its validity as soon as class begins. Each question Ms. Patterson asks about the day's reading is engaged by David, and though he isn't called on for them all, the ones he does get are answered correctly. However, while working on an in-class assignment, David suddenly feels the need to use the bathroom.

He approaches his teacher's desk and asks for permission to go. She smiles and replies, "Sure. Take one of the passes." The young boy picks up one of the wooden pencil shaped passes from the metal tray beneath the whiteboard and leaves the classroom. The hallway is quiet and peaceful, with only a few students walking through it. David enjoys the calm surroundings and leisurely walks to the bathroom. Much to his surprise, he finds the green and white room unoccupied by a single person. He chooses the fourth stall, the furthest one from the entrance, and carefully locks the door once inside it. Before sitting on the toilet seat, he wipes it down, and lines it with toilet paper.

Sitting in the small space makes the world shrink, and to pass time, he speculates about the remainder of the day. He tries to predict how the rest of his classes will go, the amount of homework he'll be given by each one, and what'll be served for lunch. While the first and second questions are significant, the third is the most important to the young boy, and like a scientist carefully observing data, David searches through his memory in pursuit of an answer to his question. He remembers the previous days' choices, recalling even the smallest details about them, but his memory of the prior week's lunches is too muddled to help him come to an answer.

Unfortunately, the sound of the door opening ends David's introspection, and his concern turns entirely to the bathroom's new occupant. He hears two sets of feet and listens closely for a voice. However, the students move throughout the room without saying a single word. The sound of their footsteps stops at the stalls, and after a few seconds of silence, it's replaced by a more familiar tune. The intimate sound causes the young boy to concentrate on relieving his own situation as quickly as possible. However, one of the boys suddenly asks, "Did you see what happened earlier?"

The question interests David, but not enough to steal his focus away. The second boy remarks, "What happened", and the first boy replies, "This guy was walking around with a piece of paper taped to his book bag. I can't remember his name though." The mention of the incident from earlier makes David's heart race, and he leans closer to the right side of the stall to better hear the conversation. Unaware of his presence, the two boys speak freely and without hesitation.

In response to the first boy's indirect question, the second says, "Oh, you mean David Parker? Yea, I saw that. What a loser." The insult cuts deeply, but David continues listening anyway. The first boy snickers and remarks, "How can someone walk around that long without realizing they've got something stuck to their back. Guess he's not very bright. I kind of feel bad for him." The two boys pause their conversation while they walk to the sinks, which gives David time to process everything he's heard. Though his peers' insults are hurtful, what's more painful to the young boy is the realization that their conversation would continue regardless of his presence.

In fact, it isn't lost on him that if they were aware of his presence, their demeanor would be infinitely more polite. Carefully crafted smiles propped up by simulated kindness and fabricated innocence would be used to give a non-threatening appearance, and their seemingly trustworthiness would draw him in like a fly, ensuring that their trap could be sprung to its fullest effect. "It's not like it was a lie", the second boy says. The first one sighs and remarks, "I mean they kind of all are. It'd be hard not to be looking like that." The second boy laughs and replies, "Most of them look like they belong in a zoo. Or maybe a toilet would be better." Despite the running faucets, David is able to understand everything the two boys say. The full weight of their words falls hard upon him, and unable to stomach it, they crush him without mercy. Tears trickle down the young boy's blank face and splash against his knees. The hope in his heart seeps out of every pore, and the sliver of strength keeping him unshakable is stamped out in an instant. As soon as the boys are out of the bathroom, David's emotions burst free, and he spends the remainder of the period sobbing in the stall.

Chapter 5

"Mr. Parker!" David lifts his head off his desk and hastily replies, "Yes?" The other students laugh, but Mr. Deene swiftly quiets them down. The young boy wipes his tired eyes and sits up in his chair. Mr. Deene crosses his arms and remarks, "Maybe you'd like to sleep in the office with Mrs. Larson?" The mention of the principal snaps David out of his daze, and he quickly replies, "No, I'm fine." The response is unconvincing, but the teacher accepts it, and returns to his lesson. However, throughout the remainder of class, he keeps a careful eye on David and the other disinterested students. The teacher's fierce gaze is noticed by the young boy, and to keep him at bay, he forces his eyes to stay open. The effort is half-hearted in appearance, but enough to satisfy the day's participation requirement. As the bell rings, indicating the end of the period, Mr. Deene turns to his students and says, "High school is only a few months away. They're not going to let you get away with as much as we do. I'll see you all tomorrow." He goes to his desk, and watches the students put away their materials and leave. David sluggishly stuffs his notebook and pencil into his book bag, and looks at the front of the classroom. The influx of students entering and exiting the class causes the doorway to quickly become congested, and not wanting to be caught in the confusion, David waits for the area to clear. After a couple minutes, a chance to leave presents itself, but as the young boy stands, Mr. Deene suddenly says, "David, can you come here for a second?"

The stern look on the teacher's face sends an anxious feeling shooting through the boy's body. David grabs his book bag and walks up to Mr. Deene's desk. The teacher folds his hands and says, "You've been having trouble staying awake during class for the past week. Have you been getting enough sleep at home?" David shakes his head and hesitantly replies, "No." The teacher reacts to his student's somber tone by softening his own demeanor. He sighs and asks, "Are you having trouble sleeping?" David nods, and Mr. Deene asks, "Have you told your mother?" The young boy shakes his head, and the teacher remarks, "If you're having problems, you need to tell someone. Okay?"

David murmurs, "Okay", and lets his gaze fall to the floor. He leaves the room and hurries down the hallway to his next class. He reaches the doorway right as the late bell rings and finds a seat in the back of the room. As the young boy sits down, Mrs. Simmons looks at the clock, and says, "Good morning class. I hope you all are doing well. Today, we'll be discussing Ancient Egypt. Take out your books, turn to page one hundred and fifteen, and begin reading." David's drowsiness is replaced by an eagerness to discuss the familiar topic, and he excitedly pulls out his book and turns to the fifth chapter.

He flips through every page in it, skimming the subtitles and colorful images under each section, but upon reaching the last page, he mutters, "That's it." Unlike the previous chapters in the book, which range from twenty to twenty-five pages long, the one on Ancient Egypt only has twelve. The lackluster information provided disappoints the young boy, but his excitement persists, nonetheless. He soaks in every bit of information the chapter gives, and finishes reading it before any of his peers. After the allotted time passes, Mrs. Simmons returns to the front of the class, and asks, "Can anyone tell me something they knew about Egypt before doing the reading?" David's hand shoots into the air, and with it unchallenged by any others, the teacher chooses him. Beaming with pride, the young boy answers, "They revolutionized agriculture."

Mrs. Simmons smiles and remarks, "Yes, that's correct. The Egyptians were one of the first people to use irrigation to water their crops. They did this by redirecting water to their fields from the Nile when it was flooding. Anyone else?" None of the other students raise their hands, and Mrs. Simmons remarks, "Alright, then let's learn some more." She turns on the projector hanging from the ceiling, and an ornate presentation appears on the screen in front of the white board. It garners disinterest from the majority of the students, but not David.

The sight of the brightly colored display only increases the boy's eagerness to talk, and as his teacher discusses each section, his impatience grows like a weed in the grass. Some of the material is familiar to him, but much of it is entirely new. The young boy soaks up every piece of new information like a sponge and uses them to fill the gaps in his own knowledge. Still, the end of the lesson is welcomed by David, and with his excitement at its peak, the boy's focus turns entirely to discussing the content of the chapter. Mrs.

Simmons unknowingly satiates his fervor by asking, "Does anyone have any questions?" David's hand enters the air first, and four more accompany it a few seconds later.

To his relief, he's selected first, and his restraint finally rewarded, he passionately asks, "Why is this chapter shorter than the other ones?" A number of eyes turn to the boy, while the rest remain fixated on Mrs. Simmons. The boy's sincere question visibly surprises the teacher, but she quickly regains her composure, and answers, "Unfortunately, though Egypt was one of the first recorded civilizations, for much of its history, it was conquered by other countries. As a result, there isn't as much to discuss about it. It does, however, have the distinction of being the only influential African country in ancient or medieval history."

Another student raises their hand, but before Mrs. Simmons can call on her, David abruptly remarks, "What about Songhai and Mali?" The interruption irritates the teacher and the other students as well, but the former reluctantly acknowledges the question, and replies, "They...were important as well, but due to their location, they were not as influential as Egypt on a global scale." The response, punctuated with a bitter undertone, is delivered in a fashion that discourages further comments. David is unfazed by it though, and another question is already on the tip of the boy's tongue. However, the bell stops him from asking it, and renders any attempt to do so futile.

The routine ring is a relief to Mrs. Simmons, and she promptly says, "We'll discuss this chapter more tomorrow. Make sure you finish reading it if you didn't during class." The students whisper and murmur among each other as they grab their things and head out of the classroom. The conversations vary, but many of them are about the teacher and student's short back and forth. Eyes follow David out of the classroom and down the hallway, and only stop after he reaches the cafeteria. Seeing the lunch line alleviates the boy's stress, and not wanting to wait long, he swiftly finds a place behind a boy wearing a black and white jacket.

Temporarily freed from the burden of class, David allows himself to concentrate on other things, and one subject in particular dominates the young boy's mind. Standing a few feet in front of him is a girl with a light blue book bag. David peeks his head out to get a better view of the girl, but she suddenly turns around, causing him to return to his original position. Nearly being caught makes the young boy's heart jump, and to keep himself calm, he takes a few deep breaths. However, the excitement brought forth by seeing her is difficult for him to suppress, and it remains with him until his turn in line comes. After grabbing his tray, David is presented with three choices: chicken salad, a slice of pizza, and a chicken sandwich.

They all look appealing to the young boy, but he picks the slice of pizza, and finishes the meal with a green apple and carton of milk. With the easy part finished, the more daunting one comes after David exits the line. He scans the cafeteria for somewhere to sit, and in the back, he notices a table with only four people sitting at it. The young boy walks past the other one, and carefully sits at the end of the long wooden table. He places his book bag next to him on the bench and takes out his phone. The mixing of the other students' conversations creates an excessively noisy environment, but he ignores it, and attends to his empty stomach while reading a book on his phone.

Halfway into the period, a loud crash suddenly echoes throughout the room, and draws the attention of all the students. The source of the sound, an accidentally dropped tray, is quickly discovered, and the middle schoolers return to their conversations a few seconds later. David goes back to reading his book, but a nearby voice catches his ear. He looks up, and after a brief search, finds the location of its source. Sitting two tables ahead of David is the girl with the blue book bag, and unlike the one in line, his view of her is completely unobstructed. The girl's picturesque appearance is a pleasant sight, and the young boy has to force himself not to stare. The opportunity is too tempting, however, and he finds himself glancing at her every few seconds.

David is careful not to get greedy though, and in order to remain unnoticed, he looks away each time it appears he could be caught. The young boy notes a different feature of the girl with every glance, and a perfect image of her takes shape in his mind after some time. To David, the girl's most fascinating features are her hair and eyes. The former is the color of milk chocolate, and flows down the back of her head like a gentle river. The latter is a multicolored canvas bursting with beauty. The way the light makes her eyes shine is even more alluring, and despite his efforts to remain undetected, he lingers on them for a moment too long.

David and the girl's eyes meet, and uncertain how to react, he blurts out, "Hi." The greeting comes out in a squeaky tone, but the girl hears it, and kindly responds, "Hi." Her reply paralyzes David with excitement, and the young boy quickly pinches himself to make sure he isn't dreaming. The sharp pain reaffirms the realness of the situation, and not wanting to let the moment pass, he contemplates what to do next. Hundreds of scenarios flash before his mind, but indecision and nervousness stop him from committing to any of them right away. Still, the potential of talking to his crush is enough to make the boy unwilling to give up, and he continues to fervently ponder how best to go about talking to her.

One scenario in particular interests David, and feeling his chance slipping away as more time passes, he decides to act it out. He picks up his book bag and tray, and moves to the table where the girl is sitting. The young boy's heart beats like a drum the entire time, but his expression conceals how anxious he truly is. The girl curiously watches him, but doesn't say anything, which somewhat puts David at ease. After placing his book bag on the floor, he looks at the girl, and says, "My name is David." The feigned confidence works. "My name is Alice", she replies.

Her response further eases his angst and propels him to continue. "I'm in your Math class, but we've never really talked before." Alice's interest piques with the mention of their shared class, and she enthusiastically remarks, "Oh, you have Ms. Nichols too. I didn't notice. Then again, I don't really know many people in that class." Her smile captivates David and melts away the remainder of his nervousness. He smiles and says, "Well, now you have someone to talk to. I won't be much help for homework or tests though." Alice laughs and replies, "Math's not my strongest subject either, and the way Ms. Nichols teaches can be a little confusing sometimes."

Thinking quickly, David remarks, "Maybe we could study together. After all, two heads are better than one." For a moment, the boy fears he has overstepped, but his concern is swiftly relieved. The young girl considers the idea for a second, and then responds, "That'd be great. I'd been thinking of asking someone, but I was kind of nervous about it." The conversation switches from class to personal interests, and David uses the opportunity to learn everything he can about Alice. The boy diligently listens to his crush's words and memorizes every detail she reveals.

The typically mundane information she provides is as fascinating to him as an undiscovered world would be to an explorer. He stores each of Alice's likes and dislikes in the crevices of his mind while simultaneously guiding their dialogue to extract more information. The process is made even more pleasing by her enthusiasm. Every time Alice smiles or laughs, David is filled with a euphoric bliss. The one-sidedness of their conversation isn't lost on the young boy, but he doesn't mind one bit. In fact, he considers her willingness to speak with him so freely a sign in favor of his romantic pursuit. However, as David becomes the subject of their conversation, Alice stops talking all of a sudden.

Her abrupt silence confuses him, and in an effort to determine the reason for it, he follows her eyes. The young girl's gaze is directed at something behind the boy, and in tracking it, he's compelled to turn around. Standing directly behind David are three boys. The one in the middle has green eyes, short dark brown hair, and an ominous smile on his face. His friends have moppy light brown hair, and similarly colored eyes. The boy in the middle crosses his arms and remarks, "You're in my seat." David glances at the bench and says, "I've been here since the beginning of lunch." The green eyed boy smirks and responds, "Well, now it's time to get up. This is our table."

Unfazed by the request, David remains sitting, and replies, "I don't see any names written on it." The witty response annoys the green eyed boy, but he doesn't let it show, and sensing the uselessness of asking again, he decides to take a different approach. He grabs David's book bag and bluntly remarks, "Either you move, or we make you." The other two boys step forward, emphasizing the severity of the threat, but David is still unconvinced. The combined pressure of not wanting to be embarrassed in front of his crush, and desperately wanting to continue talking to her underpin his defiant demeanor. In addition, the young boy is acutely aware of the growing attention the situation is gaining from the other students, and the social repercussions for responding with weakness.

To further emphasize his unwillingness to comply, he grabs the unclasped part of his book bag, and says, "Go ahead and try." David's fearlessness is a surprise to the boys, and for a moment, the two brown eyed boys consider leaving him alone. The green eyed boy, on the other hand, refuses to concede. He grips the book bag tighter, which makes David do the same. As the two boys struggle against one another, the tension between them grows little by little, and like an unpinned grenade, the explosion is inevitable. David is the catalyst for the detonation.

Impatience gets the better of the young boy, and without thinking it through, he overconfidently yanks his book bag in an effort to free it. The attempt fails, and instead of being released, the bag is ripped open. The stunning moment is punctuated by the other students, who react with silent stares, exaggerated gasps, and wide eyes. Startled by the unexpected event, the green-eyed boy finally lets go of the book bag, and watches its contents fall to the floor. The sight has the opposite effect on David, and rather than shock, it brings out an overwhelming level of sorrow. However, the emotion's hold over the boy is short-lived, and in its place fury emerges. The pile of textbooks and notebooks on the floor provides him with more than enough of a spark, and adrenaline fuels the flame within him like gasoline.

At the same time, the reservations that would typically extinguish any violent thoughts are melted away by the intense feelings circulating inside him. The final straw for David is the expression on the green eyed boy's face. His lack of remorse, and the creeping smirk forming across his face shatter the remaining inhibition the young boy has. Freed from it, his rage bursts forth like water through a broken dam, and without delay, he lunges at the three boys. Though his anger extends to them all, he targets the ringleader first.

The speed at which he moves completely astonishes them, and before the green eyed boy can react, a hard fist strikes his left cheek. He falls to the floor, but no respite is granted to him. A barrage of blows follows the first one, each more powerful than the last. So relentless is the bombardment that the green eyed boy can barely keep his eyes open. The scene horrifies the other students, but their fascination with the spectacle overpowers their desire to intervene. Unconcerned by his classmates or their opinions of him, David delivers each punch without sympathy or regret. Negative emotions supplement the fading adrenaline as the boy's power source, and to keep himself going, he draws on memories from the past.

The inferior stimulant wanes quickly though, leaving David tired and empty. The end of the beating is a relief to the green eyed boy, but the damage done to him is so great that he chooses not to move from the floor. Likewise, David looks at his own hands and nearly passes out. No longer masked by hormones, the pain in his knuckles is unbearable, and he feels regret as he looks at the raw skin peeling from them. The shifting circumstance of the scene has a sobering effect on the two brown eyed boys as well, and seeing the dismal state of their friend, they spring into action.

They surround David and force him onto his feet. Exhausted both mentally and physically, the young boy is unable to resist or free himself. Despite the two boys' mutual interest in seeking vengeance on behalf of their felled companion, there's a little bit of confusion between them about how best to do so. But not wanting to lose their opportunity, or allow David time to recuperate, they decide to carry out their revenge without any discussion. One of the brown haired boys restrains David, and the other punches him in the stomach. The young boy keels over in pain, nearly throwing up, but he wills the vomit back down his throat. "Leave him alone!"

Alice's plea draws many of the onlooking students' eyes, but the two brown haired boys ignore her completely. They continue their assault on David, standing him up, and punching him over and over again. Each blow hurts more than the last, and it takes every scrap of willpower the young boy has left to avoid emptying his stomach onto the floor. He uses the brief interlude between each blow to catch his breath and pray for an end to the beating, and to keep his mind off the growing pain in his abdomen, he counts the number of punches he successfully endures. By the time his prayer is answered, the number is up to six, and David is barely able to remain standing. Fortunately, the dean's approach has a demoralizing effect on the two brown haired boys, and they cease their attacks and back away immediately after seeing him.

The dean's sudden appearance has an equally profound impact on the spectating students, and nearly all of them go out of their way to appear oblivious to the violent scene occurring in front of them. Dean Calloway stops in front of the four boys and examines the scene: first looking at the green eyed boy, and then his friends. His eyes settle on David, who is barely able to keep himself standing by holding onto the edge of the table. The bell suddenly rings though, forcing the dean to wait till it ends to speak. The other students silently hurry out of the cafeteria, and after the last one is gone, he asks, "Would you boys like to tell me what's going on here?"

None of them say a word, but their silence is expected by Dean Calloway, and without missing a beat, he says, "Alrighty then. I guess we'll find out in the principal's office." He helps up the green eyed boy and remarks, "Can you walk?" Initially, David believes the question is for the other boy, but after raising his head and seeing the dean's angry stare pointed in his direction, he realizes it's for him. He nods and tries to push himself up using the table, but a sharp pain forces him back onto his knees. The beating's toll is finally paid, and though he struggles against it, his stomach refuses to be held at bay. Vomit shoots out of the young boy's mouth and onto the floor, stopping only after his stomach is empty.

Dean Calloway and the other boys back away to avoid the spreading ejection, and the former remarks, "Do you need to go to the nurse?" Still recovering from his agonizing heaving, David is unable to speak, and to answer the dean's question, he has to shake his head. The boy's inability to speak makes Dean Calloway sigh, and the putrid smell of the vomit aggravates his nose. Seeking to be away from the distasteful site, he turns away from David, and says, "I'll be right back. Don't go anywhere." The disgust in his voice is obvious, and as he walks away with the other boys, the young boy feels an immense amount of guilt creeping into his heart. His body and mind, though weak, are capable enough to get him off the floor.

He sits on the lunch table bench, and stares at the mess in front of him. The settled vomit sits on the ceramic floor like a puddle on a sidewalk, invading every crack and crevice it can find. More concerning to David than the unappetizing fluid, however, is his book bag, which sits in the middle of it. The ripped black bag is thoroughly soaked, and the majority of the books in it are equally unsalvageable. Yet, David is unable to take his eyes away from the pitiful sight, and attentively stares at it until the dean returns. Dean Calloway escorts the lone student out of the cafeteria and to the office.

The young boy avoids the gazes of his peers by keeping his head down, but the embarrassment is unavoidable. The dean leads him past the lobby and into an empty conference room. Dean Calloway firmly orders David to sit, and he obeys without resistance. After he settles into a chair at the far end of the long wooden table, the dean says, "I'll be back in a few", and leaves the room. The news of the fight travels across the school like a virus, entering the ears of teachers and students alike from all grades. Due to the isolation provided by the room, this reality is unknown to David, and thus his main concerns reflect this earnest ignorance.

His primary worry is his mother, and the reaction she'll have once informed of his actions. The boy's fear is heightened by his inability to tell the time, and the solitary nature of his current situation. Even his phone, which would normally be stuffed into one of his front pants pockets, is conveniently inaccessible at the moment. Wanting to give Alice as much attention as possible, and avoid being distracted during their conversation,

David put his phone in the smallest pouch of his book bag. The decision is one the young boy now truly regrets, even more so because of the uncertainty regarding the device's condition in the vomit soaked bag.

All of a sudden, the door opens, and Dean Calloway enters the room with a clipboard in his hand. He sits in the chair to the right of David, and pulls a pen out of his pocket. He places it and the clipboard in front of the young boy, and callously says, "Fill this out, and tell me when you're finished." David skims each section of the white piece of paper, and then grabs the black pen. He fills out as much of the form as he can, leaving only the section asking for the time of the incident blank, and informs the dean of his completion by sliding the clipboard and pen across the table.

Dean Calloway picks up the former and says, "Walk me through what led up to the incident in the cafeteria." David recounts the events leading up to the fight, and as he progresses through his story, the dean looks at the form to ensure it matches the written one. After he finishes, Dean Calloway places the clipboard on the table, and asks, "Why didn't you go get a teacher or come to the office?" David shrugs and mutters, "I don't know." The lackluster response annoys the dean, but instead of probing further, he asks, "Would you like to call your mother, or should I?" The boy's hesitation disappears at the mention of his mother, and he hastily replies, "I can do it."

Dean Calloway picks up the clipboard and pen, and remarks, "Alright, then let's go." He escorts David out of the conference room and further along the narrow hallway. They stop at another door on the right, and as the dean opens it, he asks, "Do you know your mother's number?" David replies, "Yes", and the two of them enter the office. Dean Calloway sits at his desk, and the young boy sits across from him. The dean moves his telephone from the right section of the desk to the center and removes the receiver from its holder. David relays his mother's number, and Dean Calloway dials it. The wait feels excruciatingly long for the dean and the student, and as the phone continues to ring, both are convinced she won't answer.

However, at the last second, the two lines connect, and a voice on the other end says, "Hello?" Dean Calloway clears his throat and replies, "Hi, is this Ms. Parker. This is Dean Avery Calloway from Cartersville Middle School. I'm calling today because of an incident that occurred between your son and some other boys." Fearful and anxious,

David listens intently while the dean talks to his mother. The young boy analyzes each one of his responses in hopes of identifying the questions behind them, but without the ability to hear his mother, he can only guess at what she's saying.

As such, when the receiver is finally given to him, he's reluctant to say anything at all. Ms. Parker detects her son's timidness and remarks, "Are you going to say anything?" Her forthright disposition makes David shiver, but knowing the consequences of staying quiet, he replies, "I'm sorry." Ms. Parker sighs and asks, "What happened?" David repeats the story he told the dean to his mother.

She listens closely to her son's description of the event and his delivery. The boy's guilt is apparent, and his fear even more so. Ms. Parker is unsurprised by her son's frightened demeanor, but it still causes her to feel unpleasant. Although her disappointment persists, his unmistakable sadness softens much of her anger, and after David finishes, she says, "Give the phone back to Dean Calloway." Unlike her initial remark, this one is delivered less sharply, and with a more sympathetic tone.

The young boy notices the difference, but continues to be cautious. He quickly returns the receiver to Dean Calloway, who puts it to his ear, and asks, "Ms. Parker, are you still there?" She replies, "Yes", and their conversation resumes. Once again, David attempts to determine his mother's questions and responses by analyzing those of the dean. In stark contrast to their first back and forth, this one is much more active. On several occasions, Calloway's responses are spirited or agitated, and a few noticeable interruptions occur as well, one of which almost results in the dean letting loose a curse.

However, the fervor is far from one sided. Unbeknownst to the young boy, his mother's sharpness is on full display on the other end of the line. While Ms. Parker acknowledges the wrongness of her son's actions, she also understands the totality of the situation involving her child. As such, she bombards Dean Calloway with questions about the other boys, their involvement in the fight, and the punishments they'll face. The dean tries to answer her questions, but when the mother finds his responses unsatisfactory, she interjects before he can finish speaking.

This causes the tension between the two parties to grow, and Dean Calloway's aggravation to increase. In a bid to regain control of the situation and keep the conversation from dragging on any further, the dean abruptly remarks, "Maybe we should schedule a meeting with the principal." Believing the suggestion to be undesirable to the mother, Calloway waits for her to finally relent. The idea has the opposite effect, and instead of reacting with apathy, she enthusiastically says, "That sounds like a great idea." The dean recognizes and accepts the failure of his ploy, but it nevertheless causes him to feel bitter. To save face and refrain from provoking any suspicion, he masks his resentment, and politely replies, "Great, I'll go get her now." He doesn't wait for Ms. Parker's reply, and immediately places the receiver next to the telephone. As Dean Calloway stands, he scowls at David and shakes his head. Completely clueless, the young boy can only watch as the man walks out of the office and wonder why his eyes are filled with so much contempt.

Chapter 6

At the insistence of Ms. Parker, the meeting is scheduled for the following day, and a brief discussion between the mother and principal results in the evening being chosen as the time for it to occur. Much to David's surprise, the punishment he receives from his mother for fighting is less severe than expected. Nevertheless, the drive to the school is still dreadful, and he's silent the entire time. The large brown brick building is a pitiful sight to David, and as his mother finds a place to park, the young boy prays for something to happen that'll keep him from having to enter the school. His prayer goes unanswered, and seeing no choice, he solemnly accepts his fate. The one silver lining is the relative emptiness of the school. Unlike earlier in the day, the building and its surrounding premises are sparsely populated, with merely a few students either waiting around or attending after school activities. In spite of this, the walk into the building is still a shameful one. David follows his mother past the front entrance and through the adjacent door leading to the office. The pair is met at the front desk by the secretary, who says, "Hi, can I help you?" Ms. Parker glances at her son and replies, "We're here to speak with the principal." The woman looks at the parent and child, somewhat lingering on the latter, and notifies the principal using a nearby telephone. A few minutes later, Mrs. Larson appears in the lobby, and greets David and Ms. Parker. She leads them to her office, which is located in the same hallway as the dean's. However, aside from that, the two rooms are completely different.

The principal's office is bigger, and as opposed to the dean's, which was only able to fit a desk a few cabinets, the former has space to spare despite containing a large desk, multiple cabinets, and a small library. Punctuating the importance of the room's occupant even more are the two college degrees on the wall directly behind the desk. The grandeur of the room is noted by David in spite of the sour occasion. However, Ms. Parker's attention is wholly on the principal, and as soon as she sits, the mother remarks, "Thank you for agreeing to meet with us Mrs. Larson. I know you have a busy schedule, and I appreciate you finding the time to fit us into it." Mrs. Larson smiles and replies, "Of course. I always enjoy talking to parents, and considering the sensitive nature of the situation concerning your son, I believed it would be best if we talked in person in order to sort everything out. Dean Calloway informed me that you were brought up to speed on the fight. Is there anything in particular you want to discuss?" Ms. Parker folds her hands and replies, "The main thing I want to talk about is how the other boys are being dealt with. According to what I was told, the other boys requested my son move from his seat prior to the fight, and ripped open his book bag when he refused to do so. Are they going to be punished for this?"

Mrs. Larson nods and replies, "Yes, what they did was reprehensible, and each has been given an in-school suspension for their participation in the fight." The response, though sincere, is unsatisfactory to Ms. Parker, and she swiftly asks, "Why are they receiving one day of punishment while David has three?" Mrs. Larson sighs and remarks, "From what I was told, David initiated the fight, and according to school policy, the person who starts a fight is typically punished the most severely." She glances at the young boy to emphasize her point, but Ms. Parker is unconvinced by the principal's argument. She looks at her son, who has his head pointed at the floor, and retorts, "Was he not supposed to defend himself? Would it have been better if he had let them beat him up?"

Unfazed by the piercing rebuttal, Mrs. Larson nonchalantly replies, "He could have told a teacher, come to the office, or simply ignored the boys. There were a number of different things he could have done besides resort to violence." Ms. Parker crosses her arms and bluntly asks, "Would you say the same thing if the roles were reversed? Would my son receive less punishment if he had ripped one of those boys' bags?" The question is unflinching, and the way in which it is expressed discourages dishonesty or disinterest.

Mrs. Larson approaches her answer with extreme caution, navigating potential responses like a soldier crossing a minefield. The pressure put upon her is compounded by the mother's unwavering disposition and her expectation of receiving an answer promptly. After another minute of inner deliberation, Mrs. Larson is sure of her response, and she answers, "Yes, if the roles were reversed, David would only receive one day of punishment, and the boys would receive three. But with all due respect, Ms. Parker, it could have been much worse. Your son nearly put another student in the hospital. His parents wanted to press charges.

Had I not convinced them otherwise, David may be in handcuffs right now." The principal's composure slightly cracks, and a bit of irritation unintentionally leaks out. She quickly seals the breach though, hoping that her budding agitation will go unnoticed.

Ms. Parker recognizes it instantly, but instead of feeding into it, she intentionally avoids doing so. In a less forthright manner, the mother remarks, "I understand the wrongness of David's actions, and I completely agree with him being punished for them. I'm simply asking that the other boys are penalized fairly as well. Because of them, my son has lost nearly all his school supplies and is missing three full days of instruction. Yet, they're only being deprived of one. How could that possibly be fair?"

Ms. Parker's unrestrained passion strengthens the persuasiveness of her words, but disregarding it, her argument is unquestionably sound. Her logical prowess leaves Mrs. Larson speechless, and unable to find any holes in the mother's analysis, she relents to it. "The school...will reimburse you for your son's damaged items. As for the punishments given to the other boys, Dean Calloway and I will...reassess them in order to better ascertain whether they are sufficient or not." The principal's continued reluctance is aggravating to Ms. Parker, but not unexpected. She considers the meeting a success, nonetheless, and her ability to convince Mrs. Larson on behalf of her son a victory to relish. With the two parties as close to agreement as possible, the meeting is promptly ended. The fatigued principal thanks the mother for her understanding, and the mother reciprocates the gratitude. No words are wasted between the two women, and apart from a short farewell, neither of them speaks to one another again. Both mother and son are drained by the affair, in spite of the latter not saying a single thing the entire time. The sun is a somewhat startling sight to David, who due to the detached nature of the principal's office believed it to be later in the day.

However, the young boy's attention swiftly shifts to the more pressing matter in front of him. The expression on Mrs. Parker's face hasn't changed at all since walking out of the school, and to David, her consistently fierce demeanor is an ominous precursor to something frightening. Hoping to get ahead of it, as soon as the two of them are in the car, he says, "I'm sorry." Ms. Parker looks at her son and asks, "Why didn't you tell me you were being bullied?" David lowers his head and replies, "I didn't want you to think I'm weak." Ms. Parker warmly remarks, "David, I would never think or say something like that. You're my son, and you always will be no matter what." The mother's statement reassures the young boy, but he continues to be afflicted by a feeling of unresolved guilt. David looks at his mother and says, "I'm sorry for fighting. It won't happen again."

Ms. Parker touches her son's face and replies, "I'm not mad at you for standing up for yourself. I just wish you had told me this was happening before now. As your mother, it's my duty to fight on your behalf, and I'll do that every time you need me to till the day I die. But I need you to work with me also. If anyone touches or insults you again, tell me, and I'll make sure they're dealt with. You and I are a team, okay?" Her words inspire hope within the boy in a way only a mother's can, and her love, genuine and warm, envelopes him like a blanket, shielding him from all sorrows in the process. Unburdened at last by his own misplaced fear, the boy smiles, and replies, "Okay."

David uses his three days of punishment to study and finish his late assignments. Unbeknownst to him, however, a conversation occurred on the second day between his mother and the principal. The early morning call was an unexpected one, but believing it to be related to the prior day's meeting,

Ms. Parker answered it regardless. The beginning of the conversation affirmed this assumption, as it consisted of Mrs. Larson relaying her decision regarding increasing the other boys' punishment. The mother was pleased to learn that the bullies were given an additional day of suspension, and after hearing this verdict, she expected the call to be ended without much else being said. However, the topic changed suddenly from the meeting to David's grades and performance in class. The shift was a little puzzling, but the devoted mother listened and engaged intently. Mrs. Larson told Ms. Parker about the concerns of a few teachers regarding her son's lackluster performance in class.

Her curiosity piqued, Ms. Parker asked, "How can I help?" Feigning care, the principal urged the worried mother to seek medical advice in order to remedy the issue. She particularly encouraged her to see whether David was suffering from an attention deficiency disorder. Ms. Parker inquired about an alternative method to solve her son's problem, but Mrs. Larson fervently denied the existence of any. The disingenuousness of her answer was recognized by the mother, but realizing the futility of arguing, she responded as if she were heeding it. Believing her guidance to be successfully absorbed, Mrs. Larson brought an end to the call without warning. Ms. Parker knew as soon as she put down the phone what the principal was attempting to do to her son, and though the mother resented her for it, she simultaneously understood its importance, nonetheless.

Buried underneath the facade of concern was a genuine problem Ms. Parker didn't want to be ignored. However, not wanting to worry her son, she approached the situation delicately. She asked David if he was having trouble paying attention in class, and the young boy answered, "Yes." The issue's validity confirmed, she followed up by asking, "Do you know why?" David was hesitant to answer at first, and only able to offer murmurs and scattered glances. As a way to encourage her son to be honest and reassure him that he was not in trouble, she remarked, "I promise I won't get mad no matter what you say."

Her pledge convinced the young boy, and his reservations removed, he said, "I have trouble sleeping sometimes?" The admission was astonishingly underwhelming, and as a consequence, Ms. Parker patiently waited for more. Nothing else came though, and realizing her son was finished, she asked, "Do you have trouble falling or staying asleep?" David rubbed his eyes and replied, "I wake up in the middle of the night a lot." The revelation caused the mother to smile, mostly due to her son's reluctance to share it, but she sympathized with him nevertheless, and said, "I can help you fix that." Ms. Parker's reaction was comforting to David, and later that same day, he was given a small dose of melatonin to cure his insomnia.

The treatment was effective, and its success was happily realized by both mother and son. With the remedy proven, it was administered to the young boy from then on, and its effects were immediate. After returning from his suspension, David's performance in class drastically improved, and everyone noticed. In addition, the boy went out of his way not to get in trouble again, and his record was spotless for the rest of the school year. However, he wasn't the only one who changed.

To ensure her son's academic and social success, Ms. Parker took a more active role in his day to day progress. Every day after coming home from work, she asked David about his day, his feelings, and the amount of homework he'd been given. For the boy, the additional attention was appreciated, and in his mother, he found a person he could confide in at any time. Her resolve was enough for them both, and with her empowering him every step of the way, the last three months of school passed by with ease. At the beginning of the school year, graduation felt like a lifetime away, but when the day finally arrived, the young boy was stunned at how quickly the time went by.

It was a momentous occasion for every student in David's class, but no one appreciated it more than him. He woke up an hour early the day of the ceremony, and spent hours preparing for it. The day brought out an equal amount of excitement from Ms. Parker, and seeing her son in such a happy mood caused all of her lingering fatigue to fade away. She prepared breakfast after showering and getting dressed, and watched with a cup of coffee in her hand as David carefully ate in his formal clothes.

Seeing her son in his cap and gown filled the mother with pride and led her to reminisce about her own life. She remembered everything it took to get to this point, the risks, the sorrows, and all the spent tears. Though, to Ms. Parker, the child sitting in front of her made every hardship worth it. It didn't take long for David to finish his food, and as he put his empty plate in the sink, he noticed his mother staring at him.

Curious, the young boy asked, "Did I do something wrong?" For a moment, Ms. Parker considered telling him what she was thinking about, but from looking at the expression on his face, she could tell he wasn't ready to hear her story yet. She felt her son still deserved an answer, and thus, simply shook her head and replied, "No, not at all." The morning necessities completed, the mother and son left, and drove to the graduation's venue, Cartersville High School.

They arrived early, and Ms. Parker dropped her son off with the few teachers who were there as well. While she found a place to park, David was led by one of the teachers to the cafeteria to wait for the other students to arrive. It was the boy's first time in the building, and as such, he used the opportunity to take in as much of it as possible. The school's enormous size captivated David, but what truly excited him was that he'd be attending it in a few months. Unfortunately, he and the teacher reached their destination before much of the building could be revealed. As they entered the large room, the former remarked, "Find the table with your name."

David expected the teacher to stay in the room with him, but she was gone not long after relaying her command. The solitude was received well by the boy, and after a short search of the room, he found a notecard with his name taped on a table near the middle of the room. As David sat down, he looked around, and muttered, "Wow." He thought back to the beginning of the year, and all of the things that had happened since then.

He remembered the good times, such as his birthday, and the bad times, like the fight. The young boy looked back upon it all with respect rather than regret. To him, each event, whether enjoyable or not, was necessary for him to reach this point. Recalling the school year also made him think about the future and everything it would hold. Although the people would mostly stay the same, a lot else wouldn't, and in recognizing this David understood the impact the next four years would have on his life. However, he viewed the future with hope, seeing it as the next step in his journey, and an opportunity to decide how the rest of his life would unfold.

After half an hour of being alone, David was finally joined by more students. The three girls were led into the cafeteria by the same teacher as before, and as she did with him, she told the girls to find their names and then promptly left. Her abrupt exit had a similarly bewildering effect on the girls as it did on the young boy, but like him, they obediently searched the tables for their names and sat once they were found. One of the girls ended up at a table near David, but no words were exchanged between them.

Their presence had little effect on the boy, who continued to pass the time by thinking of the future, but it set the tone for the rest of the arrivals. Over the next hour, students trickled into the cafeteria, sometimes individually, and other times in groups. Tables were slowly filled, and with the number of students in the room increasing, the noise experienced a similar growth. It never reached an unbearable level though, as most of the people sitting next to each other weren't well acquainted. The conversations that did occur focused on the approaching ceremony, and from them three differing sentiments could be derived. The primary attitude towards the graduation was excitement, and the students in this group saw the occasion as their chance to be rewarded for their hard work and dedication.

The secondary attitude was anxiety, and those students who fell into this category saw the grandeur of the event with apprehension instead of eagerness. The third, and least held attitude about the graduation, was indifference. This sentiment was held by both mediocre and exemplary students, who respectively considered the function a waste of time and a steppingstone to greater accomplishments. David fell in between the first and second groups, and though his exterior demeanor was calm, on the inside, he wildly shifted between excitement and fear.

This moment was one the young boy had dreamed about for years, but once it arrived, he couldn't help but feel as if he needed more time. The event was inevitable, however, and at noon, the students were gathered together by two teachers. The entire eighth grade class of Cartersville Middle School was lined up and led from the cafeteria to the doors of the auditorium. Sweat began to form under David's arms, and as the muffled music swelled nearby, his heart tried its best to free itself from his chest.

Unlike the practices, which were done with little effort in the middle school's gym, the real thing was far more nerve-racking. The young boy couldn't move, speak, or breathe without questioning the act first, and as the students slowly inched into the auditorium, his anxiety worsened. David's sentiments were anything but unique though. Each student experienced a similar emotion, albeit for a different reason. The loud music, the awkward attire, and the large crowd all contributed to the uneasiness afflicting them. In spite of this, there were positive feelings as well. For the parents in particular, seeing their child walking down the aisle in their ornate regalia brought them pure joy.

Even the angst many of the students were dealing with was equally matched in presence by pride and happiness. Reaching their seats was collectively comforting nonetheless, and with the attention they were receiving diminished, the anxious feelings disappeared for most of the students. David was unlucky in this regard, and in contrast to his peers, he continued to be plagued by anxiety for a longer tenure. Fortunately for the young boy, the fated walk that scared him so much occurred later in the program. The vice principal spoke first, addressing the parents, students, and faculty members.

Afterwards, he gave a short speech in honor of the graduating students. He commended their efforts in the past school year, motivated them to continue excelling, and sang the praises of the attending parents. The speech was refined and passionate, but sadly, the audience reacted to it with indifference. Out of a sense of obligation, they politely clapped and smiled after the vice principal finished speaking, but it was obvious how insincere their responses were. To every member of the audience, each part of the program before the certificate ceremony was simply an insignificant filler of time.

As such, the principal's speech elicited a similar reaction as his subordinate's. To everyone's relief, his speech was the final one. Ms. Nichols began the certificate ceremony by explaining its procedures and issuing a warning to the overeager parents in the audience. With the rules strictly defined, she asked the students to stand, and started calling their names. The pace of the process was steady, but to David, it appeared to move at the speed of a rollercoaster. He counted as each person ahead of him walked the stage, and tried to mentally prepare himself for his own turn, but his anxiety persisted despite this effort. Seeing no better option, he decided to face the issue head on, and valiantly began his march when his turn arrived.

To keep his hands from shaking while walking towards the stage, the young boy glued them to his sides, and he avoided the crowd's gaze as he ascended the stairs. In the middle left section of the auditorium, Ms. Parker watched her son walk to the center of the stage and accept his diploma from the principal. The sight brought her an irreplaceable joy, and seeing the smile on his face nearly made her weep. The proud mother wanted to clap and cheer, but she didn't want to ruin her son's moment by causing his diploma to be taken, and so she swiftly suppressed the urge.

Watching David walk off the stage, Ms. Parker was reminded of his birth, and how she felt that day. She was so uncertain as she held the newborn in her arms. She knew not how long he would live, what obstacles he would face, or how he would be recognized by the world. What she knew for certain was that his journey would be neither simple nor easy. Hope was all she had, and she clung to it for dear life. To the mother's delight, her unconditional love and commitment were rewarded. The child she struggled to bring into the world had excelled despite the barriers put in front of his path. He had conquered the first fourteen years of his life, and the future only looked brighter. She couldn't help it. As David sat back down, Ms. Parker cried tears of joy.

Chapter 7

"Are you sure you want to do a sport during your first year? You still haven't completely adjusted to high school." David looks at the passing scenery and replies, "I've been studying every day, and my grades are good. I can handle swimming too." His confidence is comforting to Ms. Parker, but worrisome at the same time. She doesn't want to discourage him, but she knows from personal experience how dangerous confidence could be when paired with naivete. "Why not wait till next year. Your GPA will be set, and that way you won't be under as much pressure to maintain your grades." The mother's sentiment, though sugar coated, still puts a dent in the teen's resolve. "You don't think I can do both sports and school?" His tone reveals the damaging effect his mother's words have on his pride, and wanting to soothe the wound, Ms. Parker quickly responds, "No, I'm not saying that. I just think you should wait a year before you take on more responsibilities." Nevertheless, her argument is unconvincing to David, and in a final attempt to sway his mother to his side, the teen says, "Can I at least go to the tryouts? If I'm allowed to join, I can see how much time I have to commit, and if I don't make it, no harm done." The teen's reasoning has holes in it, but out of a desire to reach a middle ground with her son, Ms. Parker concedes. "Okay, you can go to the try out. But make sure you let them know you haven't committed yet."

The compromise delights David, and he agrees to its terms immediately. Ms. Parker enjoys seeing her son in such a happy mood, but at the same time, a feeling of uncertainty regarding her decision persists. To get her mind off it, she changes the subject of the conversation by asking, "Have you made any friends?" The smile disappears from the teen's face, and he nonchalantly replies, "No." Finding the answer insufficient, the curious mother asks, "Why not?" David shrugs and replies, "I don't talk to anyone, and no one talks to me. It doesn't really bother me though."

The response worries Ms. Parker, but she doesn't allow it to be shown. She glances at her son and asks, "Who do you sit with at lunch then?" He looks away and replies, "No one; I sit by myself." His candidness, while appreciated, is disturbing, and in contemplating his response Ms. Parker finds herself unable to offer one back. Her lack of a rebuttal is noticed by David, and recognizing the jarring nature of his answer, he remarks, "It's not like these people have changed Mom. They're the same as they were last year." Ms. Parker detects a hint of resentment from her son, but in truth, it's unsurprising to her. She knew at the beginning of the school year it would be difficult for David to establish a friendship with most of his classmates, but she still encouraged him to try.

Up until this point, she had relied on her son to self-report his progress regarding the issue, but from this morning's conversation, it's obvious there hasn't been any, and Ms. Parker is unsure whether that's a good or bad thing. On the one hand, she doesn't want to force her son into an awkward situation, but on the other, she doesn't want his outlook on relationships to be tainted in the future as well. The school comes into view, and once the mother is near it, she asks, "What about that girl...Alice?"

David sighs and responds, "I don't see her a lot, and even when I do, she doesn't say much." Ms. Parker stops in the drop off area near the school's front entrance, and after switching the car's gear to park, she remarks, "Maybe you should try starting a conversation with her. Women like men who are confident." David grabs his bags and opens the passenger side door. As the teen steps onto the sidewalk, he remarks, "I'm not really that concerned about girls right now." The proclamation alarms the mother, and in a panic, she asks, "You do like girls though, right?" To David, the statement seemed harmless, but seeing its effect on his mother, he recognizes the need to clarify it. "Yea, I'm just concerned about other things right now." The explanation feels weak to the teen, but it succeeds in reassuring Ms. Parker.

She smiles at her son and says, "Okay, just making sure. Have a great day." David replies, "You too...", and closes the door. As he heads into the school, the exchange between himself and his mother reruns in his mind. Despite the moment being passed, the teen's memory of it is distinctly clear, and the longer he reflects on it, the more unbelievable the situation feels. Never before had anyone questioned David's sexuality, and even if they had, he would have never expected the conversation to feel so controversial.

More striking to the teen, however, is his mother's reaction to his initial statement and her subsequent response. He had only seen her that frightened a few times before, and by comparison, those occasions appeared a lot more dire. Furthermore, the considerable amount of relief she showed after his answer caused David to feel a similar, but unusual alleviation. The teen wonders what would have happened if he'd responded differently, but he's unable to think of an answer. He decides not to dwell on the matter, and instead turns his attention to the rest of the day. David goes to the cafeteria, where the other early students are, and finds a seat at an empty table. He notices some of his peers standing in line for breakfast, and briefly considers doing the same. However, he reconsiders the idea after remembering the last time he ate the breakfast provided by the school.

During the first week of school, David was dropped off early after waking up an hour sooner than usual. Typically, he would have eaten something at home beforehand, but on that particular day, he had forgotten. Worse yet, he realized his mistake as he was walking through the cafeteria doors. His initial solution to the problem was to wait till lunch to eat, but he recalled orientation, and the information given during it. Without giving it much thought, David entered one of the lines, and obtained a white paper bag and a carton of milk. To the hungry teen, they were like a gift sent in a time of need by a divine entity. But his exuberance faded as soon as he saw the contents of the bag. The teen was by no means expecting a luxurious meal, but the food was bad even by his own mediocre standards. It consisted of a lukewarm egg sandwich wrapped in a flimsy see through plastic bag, and a package of brown apples. In an effort to give the food a chance, he disregarded its appearance, and tried it anyway. The sandwich was bland, the apples sour, and David couldn't bring himself to finish either. From that day forward, the teen refused to eat the school's breakfast, whether starving or not.

However, hunger is the least of David's worries. The teen's mind is occupied with the swim tryouts occurring later in the day. Despite the confidence he displayed in the car, the teen's true feelings regarding the task are less certain. He first found out about the swim team during the tour of the school at orientation. As someone who enjoyed swimming from an early age, the revelation was interesting, but not enough to motivate David to join. That idea emerged when the teen saw a commercial featuring a black swimmer, and after learning more about his school's team on their website, he decided to try out for it.

To prepare, he heavily researched the sport and practiced his form at the local pool. By

October, David knew the basics of the four main strokes, and how to perform each one. Thinking his mother would support his decision, he waited a week before the try out to inform her of it. She was less enthusiastic than he had hoped though, and immediately questioned the teen about why he wanted to join the swim team. His explanation lessened her apprehension towards the idea, but she continued to voice her doubts in the following days. David countered his mother's skepticism each time, but as the try out neared, the teen's morale slowly wavered.

The same uncertainty looms over David today, but he does his best to ignore it. Luckily, the morning bell rings, signaling the beginning of the school day, and giving the teen something else to focus on. In following this, he shifts his mind completely to class, and tucks away his feelings about the try out. The school day progresses normally, with the first four classes going by slowly and the last three passing by quickly, and as usual, lunch provides David an appreciated interim to his rigorous courses. The end of the day offers a similarly satisfying feel, and after his last class, David goes to his locker.

After opening it, the teen is greeted by his gym bag, and seeing it causes his doubt to reemerge. At the same time, his phone lights up, and a reminder for the tryout appears on the screen. He looks at it, and then back at his gym bag. Both symbolize a choice for the teen, and each one comes with its own unique consequences.

He could heed his mother's advice, and wait till the next year to try out for the swim team. Not only would the decision please her, but it would also give him extra time to prepare. However, in choosing this path, there lies the possibility that fear may eventually overpower his will and keep him from attempting to join the swim team altogether. Conversely, he could confidently forge ahead, display his current prowess, and avoid the nerve-racking reality of waiting. Following this path could mean facing rejection shortly, but it could mean being accepted as well.

After a couple minutes of considering the two options, David chooses the second one. He grabs his gym bag, locks his locker, and hurries to the natatorium. In spite of the slight delay, the teen arrives with time to spare, and as he enters the pool area, the swim coach looks at him and remarks, "Basketball tryouts are next door." The statement has a jarring effect on David, but he stays steadfast, and firmly replies, "I'm here for the swim tryout. Is this the right place?" The swim coach looks at

David again, this time fully inspecting him. He skeptically peers into the teen's brown eyes with his own blue ones, but the former only offer sincerity and determination. The realization stuns the swim coach, and he brazenly asks, "You want to swim?" Without hesitating for a second, David nods and replies, "Yes." The coach's suspicion persists, but he shrugs, and says, "Alright, get changed, and show me what you've got."

His approval alleviates some of David's nervousness, and preferring not to keep the coach waiting, he hurries to the locker room. Along the way, he takes the entire space in, but his primary focus is the pool. Despite never seeing it before, the teen knew it was big, but he hadn't imagined it would look so impressive. The twenty five yard basin stretches from one side of the room to the other, and sinks twelve feet into the floor. To the inexperienced swimmer, the pool is a daunting beast, but to the initiated, it's a second home.

David watches the members of the swim team gracefully swim from one end of the pool to the other. The way they glide through the water without splashing in the slightest captivates the teen, but at the same time, it causes his nerves to return. To lessen their impact, he looks away from the pool for the rest of his walk. The empty locker room offers the teen a peaceful environment, and a much needed solitude. He walks into the bathroom area, and finds an empty stall to change in. Unlike the other swimmers, who sport jammers or speedos, David's attire is more suited for a public pool than a professional one. The contrast is acknowledged by the teen, but he decides not to dwell on it.

After filling his gym bag with his regular clothes, he secures it and his book bag in an empty locker. With nothing left standing between him and the try out, he tucks his towel underneath his right arm, and walks to the door. But before exiting the locker room, the teen takes a few deep breaths, and reassures himself for the final time. Though David's anxiety remains, it is equally matched by determination, and he uses both to propel himself forward. A cold breeze greets the partially exposed teen outside of the locker room that makes him shiver, but he powers through it, and calmly returns to the other side of the pool area.

As David walks past the diving board, the swim coach looks at him, and asks, "How many strokes do you know?" The teen turns to the pool and answers, "All of them." His confidence amuses the coach, and he smirks and remarks, "Great; do each one down and back." David fearlessly accepts the challenge, and slowly enters the pool after placing his towel down. The water is cold, but the teen quickly acclimates to the temperature, and begins swimming. He does freestyle first, backstroke second, butterfly third, and breaststroke fourth. To minimize each stroke's strain, David performs them slowly, and to compensate for his lack of speed, he prioritizes displaying his mastery of each stroke's mechanics. The endeavor tires him regardless, and it takes him more effort to get out of the pool than it did to get in. The swim coach notices the teen's exhaustion, and asks, "Have you done any sports before?" David shakes his head, and the coach remarks, "I can tell."

The comment worries the teen, and for a moment, he's overcome by a feeling of failure. However, the coach promptly says, "That was pretty good though", and his fears are lifted away. Beyond elated, David grabs his towel, and asks, "Does that mean I'm on the team?" The coach chuckles and says, "You've got a lot of work to do, but I think there's definitely a place for you on this team. What year are you?" David wipes his wet face and answers, "I'm a freshman...sir." The coach smiles and remarks, "It's Kelly, Coach Kelly. What's your name?"

David smiles back and replies, "David Parker." Coach Kelly outstretches his hand and says, "Welcome to the swim team David." He giddily shakes the coach's hand and replies, "Thank you." A sensation of victory courses through the teen, energizing his body and eliminating its fatigue. He savors the proud moment, and stores it in a vault in his mind alongside his other pleasant memories. As to not spoil the teen's jubilant mood, Coach Kelly takes it easy on him during his first practice. He has David work on the fundamentals of the freestyle stroke, which he identifies as the novice swimmer's strongest one.

In addition, the coach allows the teen to stop practicing early, choosing to use the remaining time to provide him with more information about the team. David readily absorbs it all, and leaves the pool ready to relay it to his mother. Ms. Parker picks her son up at five thirty, and before she can ask, he tells her everything. The bulk of his story is about the tryout, and hearing of her son's success overjoys the mother. However, she expresses her reservations after David finishes, and once again advises him to wait till next year.

Fueled by the euphoria of triumph, the teen courageously proclaims, "If my grades fall, I'll quit the team for good, and I won't do any sports for the rest of high school." The declaration shocks Ms. Parker, who finds it too harsh even for her. It produces a similar reaction within David, and though the teen feels some regret at making such a risky gamble, he refuses to retract it. Ms. Parker is hesitant to accept the compromise due to its finality, but she's reluctant to reject it outright as well. The deal is a much better one than she would have offered, and its terms are unquestionably in her favor.

However, from a parental perspective, she doesn't want to give her son the impression that she's willing to bargain when it comes to every single decision. On the other hand, as someone who was once in his position, she understands that her son's desire is rooted in a genuine interest, and not tied to some sort of sinister scheme. Ms. Parker takes all of this into consideration and renders her verdict with certainty. In response to his mother's decision, David hugs her, and happily says, "Thank you."

The teen treats the commitment as an unbreakable contract, and puts the sum total of his efforts into swimming and maintaining his grades. The weight of the adjustment is evident to both him and his mother, but he accepts it without complaint. In the beginning of the swim season, his grades slightly deviate, but by the middle, they're back to normal. His skills as a swimmer improve at a similar pace. As someone with no previous athletic experience, David's conditioning is much more grueling, and for the first month of practice, he comes home tired and sore. Over time though, his body adapts to the demanding workout, growing faster and stronger with each passing day.

His progress is noted by Coach Kelly, and in an attempt to draw out more of the teen's latent talent, he has him compete along with the senior members of the team. David loses four races in his first three matches, but each time he learns from his mistakes and improves. His first victory happens in the middle of December, and with it comes a glimpse of future greatness. The other members of the swim team take notice as well, and where before they were indifferent to David, as he begins to display his worth to the team, their attitude towards him drastically changes.

They become the teen's mentors, and provide him with advice about swimming, school, and life in general. Their presence has a profound effect on David, and by the end of the school year, his solitary nature is no more. The teen's transformation is most stunning to Ms. Parker, but she's grateful for it, nonetheless. David finishes his freshman year with grades that put him near the top of his class, and an optimistic outlook on the future.

Chapter 8

Mr. Xiao looks at his students and asks, "Can anyone tell me the chemical name for salt?" Most of the students are unresponsive, but a few hands enter the air. Mr. Xiao picks David's, and the teen answers, "Sodium Chloride?" The teacher writes the formula on the board and remarks, "Your first quiz is coming up, and as all of you should know, it'll be on the first thirty elements. You'll need to know each element's name, symbol, and atomic number. I'm going to hand out a review sheet Friday, and we'll have a short review session on Monday. Any questions?" A girl named Crystal raises her hand and asks, "How many questions will be on the quiz?" Mr. Xiao sighs and replies, "As of now, there are only thirty, one for each element, but depending on how far we get this week, more may be added." The students collectively groan, and Mr. Xiao remarks, "It won't be that many, and no matter what's added, we'll sufficiently review it before the quiz." His announcement soothes many of the students' concerns, and on cue, the bell rings. Mr. Xiao dismisses the students, and they gather their things and leave the classroom. David moves with less haste than his peers, and waits till he's written his homework down to begin packing. As he zips up his book bag, a girl stops in front of his desk, and says, "Hey David, do you mind studying for the quiz with me at lunch?" David looks at her and replies, "Yea, I'm free." The girl smiles and remarks, "Cool; see you then."

She walks away, and David watches her until she's out of the classroom. The unexpected encounter brightens up the teen's day, and he thinks about it while walking down the hallway. It was the first of its kind, and though David knew the girl and had talked to her a few times before, there wasn't any indication that anything further could come from those conversations. However, since the beginning of the year, David began to notice an unusual amount of attention directed his way by other students. People who had never spoken to or engaged with him the prior year suddenly started to. The teen initially treated the uptick as random, but later on, he realized something interesting. The people who were talking to him either knew fellow members of the swim team or other students associated with them. David came to this discovery two weeks ago, but until now, it had been an afterthought. However, today's encounter is different than the previous ones, and with it comes a new wrinkle. The teen's experience with girls is minimal, and as a consequence, he's unsure how to approach the situation. The memory of the last time he actively pursued a girl and the regrettable results it produced is still fresh. In addition, there exists doubt in David's mind relating to whether she has a genuine interest in him or not.

From their short conversation, it appears as though she does, but the more he thinks about it, the less sure he feels. To the teen, it's equally possible the girl could or could not like him, but he's unwilling to commit to either belief. In hopes of determining which is better to assume, he weighs the consequences of each one. Neither presumption is without its benefits and repercussions, but one doesn't stand out as better than the other. Unfortunately, his detective-like examination of the future study session is unexpectedly cut short. A tall teen with a black buzzcut bumps into David as he's walking by, and mutters, "Move, nigger." Initially, the rude shove draws the whole of the teen's concern, but he soon realizes what the other student has said, and instinctively turns arounds. "What did you just say", David asks. The tone and volume in which he delivers the question draws some of the passing students' attention, but most of them continue obliviously walking by. David's visible anger amuses the black-haired teen, and hoping to bring out more, he smugly replies, "You heard me." The bait is effective, and enraged by his unrepentant attitude, David fearlessly approaches him. However, he's careful not to get too close, remembering the consequences of his last fight. His cautiousness does nothing to hinder his other intention, and with a knifelike fury, he says, "Say it again."

The intensity of the challenge is multiplied by the unwavering way it's declared, and the two teens' shared height. The black-haired teen grins, but doesn't speak. His subtle apprehension is noted by David, and seeing it as an adequate victory, he turns to walk away. However, the black-haired teen suddenly shoves him, and remarks, "You gonna run away, nigger." Although the attack was unexpected, David is able to maintain his balance, and swiftly turns to his attacker. He drops his book bag and balls his fist, but stands firm. The teen's rage is unmistakable, but he's able to suppress his intense desire to violently respond by recalling his mother's advice. The escalating situation between him and the other teen draws more of the students' eyes in the hallway, and as a result, a crowd forms around the two of them.

While David is indifferent to the growing audience, the black-haired teen feeds off its presence. He can tell how close his counterpart is to lashing out, and how keen the crowd is to see him do so. Eager to please the other students, the teen vindictively says, "Nigger." The reactions to the revolting word vary, ranging from visible disgust to covert satisfaction, but all of the spectating students share one thing in common, shock. Where before the black-haired teen's utterance of the insult was muffled by hallway commotion, the unabashed way he repeats it in spite of the spotlight squarely on him stuns every person who hears him.

The bold action has its desired effect, and hearing the belittling term for a third time pushes David past his limit. Without saying a word, he pushes his book bag out of the way, and walks up to the black haired teen. High on arrogance and an unreal sense of security, the racist student nonchalantly watches his counterpart come closer, and as David stops in front of him, he opens his mouth to deliver another insult. However, the black-haired teen is struck in the jaw before a single word can come out. The impact of the punch is felt by every student in the area, and the hallway fills with the sounds of gasps and murmurs. Some take out their phones in an attempt to document the moment, while others soak it in naturally.

The racist student is sent to the floor by the powerful strike, and for a moment, he's unsure what's happened. The swelling lump on his lower left cheek is what clues him in, and after touching it, he shivers in horror. He looks at David and tries to speak, but the pain in his jaw is excruciating. The teen is unwilling to be unheard though, and using all of his strength, he mutters, "You...bro...my...jaw." He regrets the effort immediately and swiftly shuts his wounded mouth. David glares at the injured teen without a single drop of compassion or regret.

Were it not for his fear of facing further consequences, his first punch would have been followed by many more. Instead, the teen picks his book bag up and looks at the crowd. The other students stare at him as if he's a gladiator who just killed a mighty lion, but the picturesque scene is interrupted by the ring of the late bell, which causes many of the students to leave. However, David ignores it, and continues to loom over his downed opponent, daring him to retaliate. The black-haired teen is thoroughly demoralized though, and to avoid incurring another painful wound, he stays on the floor. His cowardice contents David but disappoints him at the same time. The teen expected more of a fight from his cocky counterpart, and in truth, he was hoping for more as well. Nonetheless, his mind is pulled away from his beaten foe by a growing noise from the outer portion of the remaining crowd.

Alerted about the fight by a passing student, two security guards hurry to the scene. They push past the students, all the while ordering them to disperse, and quickly get in between David and the black-haired teen. While one attends to the injured student, the other quickly restrains David. He doesn't resist, and allows the security guard to escort him without trouble. Thanks to the time of day, the hallways are mostly empty, and the small number of students they pass are either unaware of the fight, or only partially knowledgeable of it.

Although, the opinions of his fellow peers are far from the main thing on David's mind, and as he's silently walked to the office, the teen thinks about what'll happen next. He knows the penalty for fighting, and how much worse the punishment might be because of the injury he gave his fellow student. At the same time, the teen wonders if the events leading up to the confrontation will contribute to how it's adjudicated. The security guard leads David into the office and says, "Wait here." The teen sits on the wooden bench against the back wall, and the security guard notifies the secretary at the front desk of his exploits. After providing all the necessary details, he leaves, and she calls the dean to inform him of their new guest. The news is an unpleasant surprise to the disciplinarian, but he tells the secretary to have David continue waiting in the lobby. She relays the message to the teen, who responds to it with a quiet nod.

In spite of the less than ideal circumstances, David's mood is unusually calm. He reflects on the fight with satisfaction rather than regret, seeing his actions as a necessary statement instead of an unfortunate overreaction. The teen's familiarity with the school's policy regarding fights further fuels his unworried attitude. Though the thought of being expelled crosses his mind, David considers it to be an unlikely outcome for a first offense. Of course, he still doesn't take the idea of receiving a suspension lightly.

The teen knows how much of a negative effect such a punishment might have on his academics and participation on the swim team. In relation to the former, missing class could impact his grades, which could lead to his mother disallowing him to continue being a part of the former. Although, David is aware that his extracurricular participation could be snatched away simply because of his conduct. Neither scenario is appetizing to the teen, but he contemplates neither with fear nor anxiety. The memory of the other student's racist remark is fresh in his mind, and in it he sees all the justification needed to be acquitted of his actions by the school and his mother.

Time passes slowly in the office, with only the occasional phone call to break up the monotonous silence. The secretary attends to her duties as if David isn't there, limiting her interactions with the teen to the odd glance. However, the lack of engagement doesn't bother him. He treats the time as a break from the day's troubles and watches the clock to pass it. Twenty uneventful minutes later, David hears nearing footsteps.

The teen's first thought is that they're the dean's, but he listens closer, and realizes there's more than one pair approaching. Two police officers casually enter the office and go up to the front desk. David curiously watches them, and as they talk to the secretary, he wonders why they're here. However, their conversation with her is short, and at its end, they walk over to David. The teen is dumbfounded by the police officers' presence, and additionally so when the one on the right asks, "Are you David Parker?" The teen answers truthfully, and the officer on the left says, "Can you please stand up?" David obeys, but asks, "Why?" The police officer ignores his question and removes a pair of handcuffs from his belt. The sight alarms the teen, but before he can pose his question again, the officers violently turn him around. This makes David panic, and in response, adrenaline surges through his body, heightening his senses and increasing his fear.

He tries to move his arms, but one of the officers grabs them and forces them behind his back. He desperately pleads for an answer, but they continue emotionlessly detaining him. His hands are cuffed, his pockets searched, and his rights read. The mandatory proceedings complete, the two officers escort David out of the school and to their car. The gravity of his current predicament becomes apparent to David during the walk to the patrol car, and after he's placed in the backseat, a powerful sensation of dread cloaks him.

The rest of the day is a blur, and for the majority of that time, David is in a dazed state of mind. As the teen is questioned, he can't help but think about the beginning of the day, and how differently he expected it to end. His disoriented condition is acknowledged by the officers who question him, and out of pity, they interrogate him less aggressively than they normally would. In spite of his fractured state of mind, the teen answers their questions forthrightly. Consequently, the interrogation is short, and David is released into the custody of his waiting mother within an hour of entering the station. Seeing her son enter the foyer unharmed gives Ms. Parker an immeasurable amount of relief. When the school called her earlier in the day, she knew it could only mean something bad had happened.

However, she didn't expect to receive such terrible news, and the callous way the dean gave her the information did nothing to soothe her fears. She left work immediately, and hurried to the police station, praying her son was unscathed the entire drive. Her hope was to arrive before David was interrogated, but by the time she reached the station, it was too late. At that point, her main concern shifted to seeing her son again. Unfortunately, the reunion between mother and son is merely a mirage, and what comes afterwards is far from pleasant.

The next day, the principal called, and informed Ms. Parker of David's expulsion from the school. The decision was expected by the mother, but she still insisted on her son's innocence, pointing out the racial slurs hurled at him by the other student and the uniqueness of his response. Her pleas were disregarded, and the finality of the school's judgement was stated once more. Worse yet, later that day, she was notified that David would be formally charged for breaking his peer's jaw, and told the hearing would occur in a month's time. The teen reacted to the news with somber acceptance, and asked, "What happens now?"

Ms. Parker was uncertain how to answer, or whether to at all, but she could tell her son was eagerly waiting for a response. So, she mustered the best one she could, "We'll have to see." David accepted the answer, but the mother could tell how unsatisfying it was to him. In the face of such a seemingly hopeless situation, Ms. Parker's resolve remained strong. During her free time, she tirelessly prepared for the hearing, seeking advice from others, and conducting research of her own. In addition, she made sure David continued his studies by enrolling him in an alternative school in the town next to Cartersville.

However, she was unable to afford an attorney, and had to rely on one provided by the court. She made the best of the situation though, and worked alongside the public defender to determine the best course of action for her son. None of these preparations made the actual day any less stressful. The mother and son arrived early on the assigned Wednesday morning in their best formal wear, and entered the court alongside their counsel. The hearing began shortly thereafter, and the charge being brought against David was revealed, simple assault. With the teen's guilt irrefutable, the presiding judge saw no reason to schedule another trial, and thus decided the case would be adjudicated then and there.

After a brief recess, the hearing resumed, and the defense and prosecution presented their arguments regarding the severity to which they believed the youth should be punished. The former sought three months in juvenile detention, and the latter lobbied for community service. The judge listened diligently to both sides, but in the end, chose neither. Instead, he sentenced David to six months in juvenile detention, citing the need for the teen to understand the significance of his misdeed. The verdict shocked everyone in the court.

Ms. Parker nearly fainted, and David's knees wobbled uncontrollably as his worst fear suddenly became reality. The judge offered no sympathy to the distraught mother and son, and continued detailing his sentence while they wept.

As David was taken into custody, Ms. Parker let out a cry that shook the soul of every person in the building, and her son responded with a plea that would make any mother cry. After being processed, David was transported to his new home a few days later. The news of the teen's arrest spread throughout Cartersville like a raging wildfire. Many saw it as a tragedy, while others couldn't care less. Some were overjoyed by it, considering the black teen's demise a victory to be remembered.

Chapter 9

Ms. Parker enters the lot and searches for a space to park. The foggy weather gives the effort an extra degree of difficulty, but the mother diligently searches for a spot regardless. The substantial difference in the number of people visiting doesn't help either. Usually, the crowd, while substantial, isn't large enough to occupy the entire parking lot. Yet today, it appears as if not even the least appealing spaces are left empty. To anyone else, the scene would be dispiriting enough to encourage them to wait till another day to visit. Ms. Parker, however, is unwilling to let such a small obstacle stand in the way of seeing her only son. She carefully circles the parking lot again, and sees a car slowly inching out of its space. Reacting quickly, the mother stops, and patiently waits for the person to vacate the parking space. Aware of his fellow driver, the old man steadily guides his dark blue sedan into the driving lane, and out of the lot. Ms. Parker immediately parks in the formerly occupied spot and breathes a sigh of relief. She looks at the gray fortress-like building, and takes a deep breath. Despite visiting the detention center numerous times, a sensation of dread latches onto her every time she prepares to enter it. Ms. Parker ignores it as she normally does, and grabs her purse and gets out of her car. An unexpected breeze flows between the mother's legs as she steps onto the sidewalk, and in response, she hastily buttons up her coat.

She walks along the weathered concrete pathway, and past a set of glass doors. Inside the building, the mother is welcomed by guards, an old scanner, and a metal detector. She greets the two men, and they reciprocate the acknowledgment. The taller of the two, a bald black man with dark brown eyes, politely asks the mother to place her things in the tubs beside the scanner. The request is a familiar one, and as always, she complies without issue. After the two gray tubs are filled with her purse and the contents of her pockets, the guard instructs her to walk through the metal detector.

Ms. Parker passes through the gray machine without setting it off, and retrieves her things from the tubs on the other side of the scanner. After readjusting herself, she goes to the line for visitation, and settles behind a young girl holding a baby. As the mother waits, she scans the faces of the people standing in front of her. Some are recognizable, but many more are new; an observation that Ms. Parker reflects on solemnly. The line's pace is steady though, which prevents her from dwelling on the grim reality for too long. As the clerk's desk comes into view, the baby in front of Ms. Parker suddenly waves at her. She returns the friendly gesture and happily whispers, "Hi, how are you?" The beautiful baby boy smiles, and Ms. Parker can't help but do the same. She waves again, and in response, the baby lets out an adorable laugh.

The young woman notices the noise coming from her child and turns around. Ms. Parker smiles at her and politely says, "Sorry, he's just so cute." The young girl smiles back and replies, "Oh, it's okay. Thank you." Ms. Parker sighs and asks, "What's his name?" The young girl looks at her child and replies, "Malachi." Ms. Parker nods and remarks, "Such a beautiful name." The baby reminds her of David, even more so due to him bearing a similar appearance to her son when he was the same age. The infant's brown eyes are a shade lighter than David's, and his skin is only a touch darker. Looking at the child awakens Ms. Parker's dormant thoughts, and she's bombarded with memories of when her son was a baby. The mother's recollection of the monumental period in her life is clear, but it feels like the memories are from a lifetime ago rather than merely a little over ten years. It's as if they're located in a reality far removed from the one she's currently in.

"Who are you here to see?" The question brings Ms. Parker back to the present, and she replies, "My son. Are you here to see your brother?" The young girl looks at the baby, and shyly responds, "His father." The smile disappears from Ms. Parker's face, and she remarks, "Oh...that's great." In spite of the mother's efforts to mask her astonishment, the effect of the young girl's reply on her is glaringly evident. However, she takes no offense at Ms. Parker's shock, and offers her a cordial smile.

With the conversation between the two women at an uncomfortable juncture, they silently agree to let it come to an end. The girl turns around, but Ms. Parker is unable to shake her disbelief regarding her. She noticed the resemblance between the baby and young woman right away, but due to the girl's juvenile appearance, she assumed they were siblings. But the answer she gave to Ms. Parker's final question, while somewhat vague, revealed the true nature of their relation to one another. Her first idea after hearing the girl's answer was to ask her age, but she decided not to engage in that type of inquiry so as not to be perceived as rude.

There was no real need to ask anyway, as Ms. Parker was able to place the girl's age at either seventeen or eighteen. Nevertheless, the encounter becomes an afterthought once she reaches the front of the line. As the mother steps up to the clerk's desk, the middle aged woman standing behind it asks, "Who are you here to see?" Ms. Parker swiftly answers, "David Parker", and the clerk types the name into her computer. A profile of the teen appears on the screen, and she scans it for any irregularities. Nothing stands out, however, which prompts the clerk to say, "Please fill out all of the information on one of the sheets below."

She points at the bulky black binder in front of her, and Ms. Parker picks up the pen beside it and fills in one of the empty lines. After she finishes, the clerk says, "Alright, your visit today will be non-contact. Please proceed through the adjacent hallway to the visitation area." Ms. Parker thanks her and enters a narrow corridor on the right side of the room. She follows the passageway to a small gray room with two doors, and walks over to one of the cushioned chairs against the right wall.

The other people in the waiting area acknowledge the mother's presence, but quickly return to what they were doing before. As Ms. Parker sits, she takes a deep breath, and looks around the room. Due to the frequency of her visits, the mother is well acquainted with the waiting area, and as always, a grim air pervades the space.

To lighten things up, she examines the room every time she comes to the facility to see if it's changed at all. The results of the game are often minute, with cracks, chipped paint, or loose carpet fibers typically being the new details discovered, but it's barely engaging enough to distract Ms. Parker from the depressing predicament she's in. Today's observations are easy to make: an additional chair and a guard posted in the left corner of the room. Both additions are interesting, but the latter intrigues the mother the most.

As far back as she could remember, there had never been a guard in this section of the building, which naturally led her to wonder why there was one now. Was it simply a harmless measure added to further improve the safety of the facility, or had a violent incident occurred that elicited the need for more security. Either way, it adds another solemn layer to the already somber situation. All of a sudden, the door on the right opens, and the young woman from before walks into the room. She and Ms. Parker notice one another straightaway, and the two women offer each other a weak smile. Nothing is said between them, however, as the young woman leaves without pause. A second later, a bearded guard walks into the room and announces a name. A man in a maroon sweater responds and follows him through the right door. As soon as he walks past it, the door is closed, and the room rendered silent again.

Ms. Parker eagerly stares at the left door, wishing with each passing second that her turn will come soon. The absence of a clock in the room makes the wait all the more agonizing. Seconds turn to minutes that feel like hours, and each time someone enters or exits one of the doors, Ms. Parker's patience is further strained. Thirty minutes after the mother's arrival to the room, the door on the left opens, and a guard finally walks out and says, "David Parker." The mother swiftly gets out of her chair, and remarks, "That's me." She walks through the door, which is quickly closed by the guard, who escorts her to the visitation area afterwards.

The large well-lit room is divided by a white brick wall. On one side, juveniles are brought in through a set of metal doors, and on the other, family members enter tiny booths and wait on uncomfortable stools to see them. The two parties are separated by thick glass partitions, with only a pair of black phone receivers as a means of communication. Under normal circumstances, the abysmal arrangement would be anything other than appealing, but to those starved of interaction with the people most important to them, it's more than adequate.

For a mother who can only see her son once a week, the setup is an eagerly accepted concession. Ms. Parker sits at the empty booth in the back of the room and places her purse on the counter. The doors on the other side of the room open, and David is walked in by a guard and directed to the booth across from his mother's. Seeing her son puts a smile on Ms. Parker's face, but the delight of the sight is slightly ruined by the yellow jumpsuit on the teen's body. Nonetheless, she smiles as her son sits in front of her, and impatiently grabs the receiver next to her.

In stark contrast, David acts less enthusiastic about speaking to his mother. The expression on his face is one of misery, not joy, and he reaches for the receiver beside him with a noticeable amount of hesitation. However, Ms. Parker brushes aside the ominous observation, and says, "David." The teen whispers a response, but the mother is unable to hear it. She brings the receiver closer to her ear, and asks her son to repeat himself. David clears his throat and weakly asks, "When can I come home?" Ms. Parker moves the receiver away from her face and looks into her son's eyes. They convey fear, which unfortunately, is nothing new. Ever since she started coming to the facility, the mother noticed the growing pain emanating from her son's eyes. He would rarely go into detail about the suffering he faced, but through peering into his eyes, she was able to get a sense of what he had to endure.

The question he's posed isn't new either. In fact, after his first month at the detention center, David had asked the same thing every time his mother visited. Being the caring mother she is, Ms. Parker dutifully answered every time despite knowing he would be unsatisfied. Today is different though. Prior to today, he would ask that question at the end or middle of their conversation. In addition, his eyes reveal an emotion worse than pain, hopelessness, one the mother prayed she would never witness in her son.

Seeing him in such a deteriorated state brings Ms. Parker to the brink of tears, but for his sake, she doesn't let any loose. Instead, she takes a deep breath, moves the receiver back to her ear, and calmly replies, "Four months." The answer strips a large portion of the resolve left in David, and he sighs and remarks, "I can't do it anymore." The statement is a more candid one than typically given by the teen, but Ms. Parker can tell exhaustion is the reason for it. His lethargy was apparent from the moment he sat down, but the most striking sign of the teen's fatigue are the bags under his eyes. To the mother, it seems as if her son hasn't slept since the last time she visited him, and eager to know why, she asks, "Have you been getting any sleep?"

The teen rubs his eyes and replies, "When I can." The lacking answer is unsurprising to Ms. Parker, and though she understands her son's reluctance to divulge certain information, she's unwilling to ignore such an evident concern when it's right in front of her. To get the teen to answer more thoroughly, she assumes a firmer tone, and asks, "Why?" David's wariness persists, but the teen is smart enough to know the consequences of withholding information from his mother.

Furthermore, he recognizes that her interrogation of him is done purely out of love. "If I sleep, they'll attack me. I have to stay up to fight them." Though better, the answer is still a little confusing to Ms. Parker, and so she asks, "Who's doing this to you." David sighs and replies,

"Everyone. Sometimes it's the boys in my room, and sometimes it's others." The revelation shocks Ms. Parker, and seeking to know more, she asks, "How long has this been going on?" David sighs and answers, "Since the beginning." The effects of talking about the subject are distinctly visible on the teen. His hands twitch in such an intense way that it appears as though the receiver may fall out of his hand at any minute.

His knees bounce up and down underneath the counter, creating a subtle thumping sound that can be heard throughout the room, and his eyes erratically scan the area as if expecting something to suddenly happen. Ms. Parker is able to easily detect these tics, and though they worry her enough to consider moving on to another topic, they simultaneously motivate her to dig deeper. The mother's trust in her son is unshakable, but his willingness to withhold such important information makes her wonder if he's hiding anything else. "Have you told anyone, like the guards?" To her the question is harmless, but to the teen, it is painfully insulting, and he angrily replies, "They don't care! They let it happen!"

The outburst alarms everyone in the room, but the person most shaken by it is Ms. Parker. Never before had her son yelled at her. At worst, he would back talk a little, but even during those times, his voice would remain relatively calm. This, however, is something entirely different. She can feel the teen's rage from the other side of the partition, and for a moment, she's genuinely scared of her own child. David notes the fear in his mother's eyes, as well as everyone else's in the room, and regains his composure. He takes a deep breath and apologizes. Ms. Parker accepts it and says, "I didn't mean to make you upset. I just don't want anyone hurting you."

David shakes his head and mutters, "I just want to go home. I don't want to be here anymore." The sorrow in the teen's voice strains the mother's heart, and she has to force herself not to cry once again. However, the teen isn't content with silence, and impatiently waits for his mother to say something reassuring. Unfortunately, Ms. Parker has no encouraging words to offer, not even a lie. But her son continues to wait, because the only thing keeping him remotely sane is his mother's love, and she knows it. "You have to be strong. We'll get through this together. I promise."

It's the best Ms. Parker can give, but she knows it isn't enough, and she feels guilty for her inability to adequately console her son. David is appreciative of the attempt though, and remorsefully remarks, "I'm sorry. I'm so sorry. I should've listened to you. It's all my fault." A tear trickles down the teen's face. He wipes it away with his right hand, and places the other one against the partition. Ms. Parker fares no better. The sight of her son crying is too much for the mother to bear, and a second later, her own face is full of tears. She places her own hand against the partition, in the same spot as David's, and says, "Everything's going to be okay. Everyone makes mistakes. We're going to get through this, but you can't cry. You have to be strong."

The teen takes a deep breath and wipes the loose tears from his face. Ms. Parker does the same, but as she finishes, a guard walks behind David, indicating the end of their time together. The guard orders the teen to stand, and he complies immediately. Ms. Parker stands and watches as her son is taken out of the room. As he's walked to the doors, she frantically yells, "I love you! I always will." The mother's declaration is muffled by the glass, but David is able to make it out, and right before he's taken out of the room, he turns to her and mouths, "I know. I love you too."

And with that, he's gone, returned once more to the bowels of the detention center. Exhausted, Ms. Parker sits and lets her head fall into her hands. Deprived of her beloved son for another long week, the mother weeps until she has no more tears to cry.

Chapter 10

The four months progress slowly for both mother and son. Each visit is worse than the last, with more and more of the teen's will stripped away the further into his sentence he goes. By the time David's released into his mother's custody, he's a shell of his former self. The once fiercely determined child is reduced to a mere husk whose sole motivation in life is survival. Despite her son being unrecognizable, Ms. Parker refuses to give up on him. The mother picks up the pieces of her broken child, and does everything she can to put them back together. To start, she re-enrolls David in the school he was attending prior to his confinement. However, the transition is challenging for the teen. He finds it difficult to learn new concepts, and harder to recall old ones. His learning impairment is worsened by the erratic sleep pattern he developed during his time at the detention center, and as if things couldn't get worse, the teen's time in confinement increases his violent tendencies rather than reduces them. If not a part of a fight, David is the cause of it, and due to his delinquency, Ms. Parker becomes familiar with both the principal and dean in a short amount of time. As a result, the teen's first year back is a disaster, with him barely passing his classes. These initial setbacks, while daunting, are not enough to stop the mother from making sure her son succeeds. To address David's anger issues, Ms. Parker forces him to go to Dr. Mayne, a local black therapist.

The teen resists the therapist's attempts to burrow into his mind, and for a month, he answers his questions either vaguely or not at all. However, each session is an improvement on the last, and David's level of comfort gradually increases the more of them he attends. After two months, the teen's secretive disposition is overcome, and his inner struggle exposed. He reveals the horrible truth of his six months in confinement, and the mistreatment he faced during it. David describes the physical, verbal, and sexual abuse inflicted upon him by the other juveniles, and to a lesser extent, the detention center's staff. He recounts times when he ferociously resisted this mistreatment, and times when he was too tired to fight back. Confronting the traumatic memories is far from simple, and getting the teen to understand the corrosiveness of suppressing his agony is in itself a struggle for Dr. Mayne.

Some sessions are peaceful, filled with smiles and gentle conversation, and others are chaotic, dominated by tears and angry yells. But by the middle of the summer, David's progress is undeniable, and recognized by all involved parties. Though his anger and sorrow continue to be present, his control over them is much better, and the teen's infatuation with conflict is eliminated altogether. The one issue that's left unresolved by this time is David's unwillingness to confide in his mother, and seeing it as the logical problem to tackle next, Dr. Mayne directs the sum of his efforts to it.

Through careful questioning, he's able to learn the reason behind David's distrust of his mother. Contrary to the therapist's assumption, the teen's secretiveness is not rooted in mistrust, but self-loathing. He discovers that David blames himself for his confinement, and as a result, feels unworthy of his mother's sympathy. Adding to the teen's self-contempt is a concern regarding her reaction to learning about the things he suffered, and this dilemma manifests in two distinct ways. He worries about the negative effects of telling his mother the vile things that happened to him, believing they will lead to her becoming consumed by guilt and depression.

An equal fear of the teen is how he'll be perceived afterwards, and the potential of his mother being ashamed of him for being sexually abused. Though David evades many of his therapist's questions relating to the latter of the two concerns, the trained professional is able to determine the rationale responsible for it. In the teen's mind, the violations he faced are his own fault, and a reflection of his inability to protect himself from harm. Furthermore, the fact the depraved acts were done to him by other males causes David to question his sexuality, something he believes his mother will do as well.

With the problem sufficiently dissected, Dr. Mayne moves on to solving it. He approaches the issue delicately, and tenderly tries to convince David he isn't to blame for being abused, and that his mother would never be ashamed of him for it. It takes less time to persuade the teen of these things, but a significant amount of coaxing to do so. However, David's acceptance comes with a considerable demand, a session including his mother, wherein the lone topic of discussion would be the abuse he faced. Dr. Mayne agrees to the request in spite of his reservations regarding it, and the meeting is set for the following week. The session is on David's mind up until the moment it occurs, and as he and his mother enter the therapist's office, the teen momentarily considers calling it off. The thought is fleeting, however, and seeing Dr. Mayne reminds him of the meeting's necessity.

The therapist begins the session by informing Ms. Parker of her son's progress since their last talk, which she responds to enthusiastically. He follows up this announcement by detailing the subject of their recent sessions, while being careful not to reveal too much information, and Ms. Parker responds to this news in a similarly positive way. With the mother sufficiently primed, Dr. Mayne reveals the purpose of their meeting, and allows David to take center stage. The teen is terrified, but he courageously forges ahead, and tells her everything.

He details his abuse, his feelings regarding it, and explains why he withheld this information from her. Ms. Parker does not immediately respond, which gives David the impression that she's embarrassed of him. However, to the teen's surprise, his mother suddenly hugs him, and says,

"I'm sorry. I never meant to make you feel that way." The unexpected apology wipes away David's fright, and brings tears to his eyes. Unburdened by the weight of silence, he hugs his mother, and replies, "Thank you." They spend the rest of the session crying and hugging one another, and Dr. Mayne is content to let them.

Regaining the ability to confide in his mother has a rejuvenating effect on David and instills a fresh sense of purpose in his life. In a similar way, learning of her son's inner turmoil and the hardships he endured in confinement galvanizes Ms. Parker even more. These new outlooks coincide with the beginning of the teen's Junior year of high school, and the second phase of his mother's plan. Unlike the previous year, where she monitored David's schooling from a distance, Ms. Parker substantially increases her supervision of the teen's academic progress.

From the start of the school year to the end, she checks his grades at the beginning of each day, and makes sure all of his assignments are completed by the end of it. David eases the stress of the situation by working hard and completely cooperating. In spite of these commitments from mother and son, there are still disagreements between them. At times, David is aggravated by his mother's overbearing behavior, and vice versa, Ms. Parker is unsatisfied with the nonchalant attitude her son has every so often. However, their teamwork and dedication are effective nonetheless, and as a result, the school year is a massive improvement on the last one.

Rather than skating by, David comfortably passes his classes, and earns his first B since returning to school. The teen is rewarded for his hard work with a carefree summer. Besides therapy, he spends his vacation reading, playing video games, and after a gentle nudge from his mother, looking at careers as well. Before entering high school, the teen had seldom thought about what he wanted to do after it. As a child, writing seemed like a worthy pursuit, but with age came the realization that such a career would be impractical.

During his tenure at Cartersville High, the topic was examined more frequently, but not enough to produce anything tangible. The subject became absent entirely from the teen's thought while he was confined, and a distant remembrance following his release. However, with his final year upon him, the question is an unavoidable one that must be answered. By the end of the summer, David's research yields three paths: construction, engineering, and teaching. He presents the results to his mother, and she responds to them truthfully. She highlights the difficulty he'll have pursuing a career in either of the three sectors, but assures him that she'll be supportive of him no matter which path he chooses.

The final year of high school is the hardest for David, but he perseveres, and further academically improves. Other than the occasional break, the teen spends his time studying and planning for the end of the school year. His efforts are aided by his mother, who encourages him along the way, and does a bit of research on his behalf. The year passes swiftly, and graduation arrives in the blink of an eye. The end of the school year is a relief to David, who by then is beyond exhausted. His grueling devotion pays off handily, earning the teen a report without any Cs, and the right to graduate. David takes pride in the former, but he's unconcerned with the latter. Though he considers graduating an achievement, the grandeur of the event is spoiled by his advanced age.

Although David isn't the only nineteen year old in his class, or the oldest, the circumstance still gives the occasion a sour feel. Ms. Parker has the opposite attitude towards her son's graduation. She sees it for what it is, an accomplishment some are not fortunate enough to attain. The mother celebrates her son's completion of high school by taking him out to a fancy restaurant, which David refrains from complaining about despite his jaded view of the ceremony. The graduation itself is mundane, and though Ms. Parker maintains her excitement all the way through it, anyone looking in could tell her sentiment is unshared by the majority of the crowd.

Even during the portions of the ceremony allotted for claps and cheers, the collective noise is barely able to breach the exterior of the auditorium. The blandness of the event isn't helped by its speakers either, who deliver their speeches as if they're being held at gunpoint. For his mother's sake, David smiles for the duration of the ceremony, and enthusiastically accepts his diploma. As with her son's eight grade graduation, Ms. Parker cries as he walks across the stage, and showers him in hugs and kisses when they're reunited.

The mother is beyond proud of her son, not only for finishing his studies, but also for doing so in spite of the adversity he faced along the way. To see her son succeed in such a spectacular way gives her a bliss matched only by his birth. David appreciates the praise his mother gives him, but most importantly, he cherishes her undying love and unfathomable dedication. If not for her, the teen would have given up long ago, and reaching this point would have been impossible without her support. For the mother and son, the future is a bright shining star waiting to be plucked from the sky, and nothing can stop the two of them from grabbing it.

Unfortunately, the pleasant feelings are short lived, and quickly replaced by anger, despair, and emptiness. Unbeknownst to Ms. Parker, the stress she has incurred over the years has slowly taken a toll on her body, and after four years of dealing with a staggering quantity of it, her body finally reaches its breaking point. A week after David's graduation, Ms. Parker is abruptly struck by a heart attack in the middle of dinner.

The unexpected attack sends the mother to the floor with her hand on her chest. The sudden seizure alarms David, and he quickly rushes to his mother's side. The teen's initial thought is that his mother is choking, but after seeing her hand tightly grabbing at her chest, he realizes the situation is much worse. He runs into the other room and uses his phone to call for help, but when he returns, his mother is unconscious.

In a panic, the teen tries to wake her up by shaking her, but she remains unresponsive. The paramedics arrive shortly thereafter, and swiftly transport Ms. Parker into an awaiting ambulance. En-route to the hospital, the mother's heart stops, and she isn't resuscitated until they reach it. After Ms. Parker is stabilized, one of the doctors updates David on her condition. The teen is relieved to learn of his mother's successful resuscitation, but mortified by the news that she's in a coma. Clinging to hope, he asks the doctor what the chances are of her waking up, and she tells him that they're slim. She further informs the teen that she will be mentally incapacitated if she wakes up. Without a moment of hesitation, David decides to allow his mother to peacefully pass.

The choice is a heartbreaking one for the teen to make, but he refuses to let his mother live in agony, or subject her to a painful existence to satisfy his own selfish desire. At the age of forty-three, Alicia Parker is mercilessly snatched from the Earth, and sent to the ancestral plane. Her death splits David's heart in two, and crushes his resolve to pieces. His misery is magnified by the stress that comes with arranging his mother's funeral and handling her affairs.

Thanks to Ms. Parker's preparedness, much of the burden her son has to contend with relates to the minor details of the ceremony. The event is dreadful nonetheless, and with no other family members to lean on for support, the teen is forced to attend his mother's funeral alone. He receives condolences from teachers, peers, and even his former therapist, but none of it is enough to dull his pain. Sadly, the headaches continue after the burial, and before David can catch his breath, he's faced with another issue, the house in Cartersville. Having no source of income, the teen is unable to stay in the home he grew up in, and with no other alternatives, he's forced to move out of Cartersville. Leaving the town he spent his entire life in is hard enough, but being incapable of keeping the house he and his mother made so many memories in is a much crueler pill to swallow. However, the mentally battered teen accepts the bitter reality imposed upon him, and searches for a new place to call home. A month later, he moves to the city of Chicago with hopes of beginning again. But the past lingers, and wraps itself tightly around David, refusing to let him go.

Chapter 11

David scans the barcode on the back of the can of baked beans and places it into an empty plastic bag nearby. Its price briefly appears on the register's screen, before being replaced by the total cost. David tells the amount to the awaiting woman, and she hands him a crisp fifty-dollar bill. The young man opens the register drawer and places the bill in the rightmost slot. He types in the paid amount, and the machine automatically subtracts it from the total cost. He glances at the screen, retrieves the woman's change from the register drawer, and gives it to her along with a receipt. The routine is mundane and robotic, but he prefers it to the alternative, not having one at all. The job isn't his first. After arriving in Chicago, the young man found employment as a fry cook. The work was hard and low paying, but it allowed David to set himself up in the city. It wasn't the sum of his ambition though, and thus, eight months later, he sought a new employer. He landed at a clothing store as a clerk after a week of searching. The pay was better and the hours more manageable, but due to a foolish mistake, his tenure at the job wasn't long.

His next job came after an extended break, and unlike his attitude towards his previous position, the young man made it his mission to keep this one as long as possible. His efforts were in vain, however, as he was fired a mere week in. However, he didn't allow this to deter him, and urgently resumed the search for another employer. It took a few weeks, but he finally secured a job as a grocery store cashier. There was doubt in the young man's mind whether his position would last long, but with no issues a month in, he became convinced his fortunes had finally turned.

The next customer in line approaches the register, and as David grabs the first item on the conveyor belt, he suddenly hears, "David, can I see you for a moment?" He looks up and sees his manager standing by the door to his office. His first instinct is that he's done something wrong, and in an effort to identify the mistake, he recalls his day at work up until this point. However, nothing comes to mind other than memories of an ordinary day.

Regardless, the manager's request isn't optional or up for debate. David turns to one of his coworkers and asks, "Do you mind covering for me Carol?" She replies, "Sure", and takes his spot behind the register.

He thanks her, and walks over to his manager, a twenty seven year old Irish man named Paul Stralousky. Other than cordial greetings at the beginning or end of the work day, and the occasional delivery of a task, the two rarely spoke to one another. In fact, the most the manager had ever said to David was during his interview. Though, this never bothered the young man, primarily because he was far more worried about keeping his job. In this moment, David has the same concern, but so as to not arouse suspicion, he acts as if the occurrence is routine.

He calmly walks into his manager's office, who closes the door after entering behind him. As Paul sits at his desk, he remarks, "You can go ahead and sit down", and David carefully sits in the chair across from him. The office looks practically the same as it did when he was interviewed in it. Besides the additional picture frames, the small room is still filled with file cabinets, marked calendars, and miscellaneous items strewn callously around the corners. On the right side, directly adjacent to the door, is a bookshelf full of pictures, and hanging on the wall behind the desk are awards and degrees. The furnishings make the room appear larger than it truly is and give it an imposing feel. "So, you were arrested two years ago?" The temperature in the room drops by a hundred degrees, and David's body turns to lead. He tries to respond, but the words get stuck in his throat, causing him to cough. No pity is taken on the young man by his manager, who patiently waits for a response from his subordinate. David gathers his thoughts and replies, "Yes, I was." Paul sighs and remarks, "This wasn't mentioned on your application."

The way the comment is articulated suggests that an explanation is unneeded, but the expression on the manager's face says otherwise. As such, David says, "It was a mistake, one I regret to this day, but it doesn't reflect who I am now. I only left it off the application because I was worried about being hired." Paul evades his subordinate's response, and asks, "Would you mind telling me how this incident occurred?" The invitation is one David regards with suspicion, and for good reason. By disclosing the intimate details of the situation that led to his incarceration, he leaves himself vulnerable to the whims of his manager. There also lies the possibility that his superior already knows the cause of his imprisonment, and is simply testing him. Either way, refusing Paul's offer would inevitably make him look worse than he already does. Still, he's careful to painstakingly think over his answer before replying to reduce the chances of him saying the wrong thing or giving the wrong impression. It takes David two minutes to finish compiling his thoughts, by which time Paul is irritable, and anxious for some sort of answer. Sensing his superior's growing aggravation, the young man doesn't delay any longer.

He replies, "At the time, I was working as a clerk at a clothing store. I was helping a woman look for a pair of pants when a man approached me and asked for assistance. I told him I would be able to assist him in a few minutes, but it ended up taking longer than I expected to help the woman. The man angrily returned, and demanded that I stop helping her and attend to him instead. I told him I would come straight to him after finishing with the woman, but he wouldn't accept that. He cursed at the woman, and then at me. I politely asked him to wait again, but he continued to curse at me. I became agitated, and the man noticed and asked me if I wanted to fight him. I asked him to leave, and he insulted me and mentioned my mother. I snapped, and things escalated from there. It was a mistake, one I regret to this day, but I'm a changed man. I used those two years to work through my own issues and learn how to handle situations like that one."

Paul emotionlessly absorbs David's story, but provides no immediate reply, which worries the young man. Whether true or not, it feels as if his future depends on his manager's reaction to his story, and this belief intensifies the longer he goes without saying something. The suspense is excruciating, but David refuses to say another word till Paul does, and five full minutes slog by before the manager finally speaks.

"While I understand how frustrating a situation like that can be, your conduct was beyond inappropriate, and I can't risk something similar happening here. In addition, it's against company policy to lie on an application, especially when it's about something as serious as this. If you had let me know about this during or after our interview, we could've discussed it and gone from there. You didn't though, and unfortunately, I'm going to have to let you go because of that."

The decision is one David can't accept, and yearning to change it, he fiercely says, "I've changed. I'm not the man I was back then. I've served my time. Please, at least give me a chance to prove myself." If not for his pride, the young man would beg on the floor, and if his manager told him doing so was the only way to keep his job, he would do it in a heartbeat.

Sadly, Paul's judgement is set, his mind unmovable, and David can plainly tell the pointlessness of trying to convince him otherwise. Despite the mutual understanding between the two men, the manager feels the need to explicitly declare his sentiments. "I'm sorry David. I wish there was more I could do, but I just can't let this slide. I appreciate all the hard work you've done here, and I hope you're successful in your future endeavors." The remark salts David's wound, and leaves an unpleasant taste in his mouth. The energy is drained from the young man's body, and his ability to speak is rendered defective.

David leaves the office, and trudges out of the store, desperately hoping the firing will be revealed to be either a joke or dream. However, the further he gets from the store, the more the finality of the situation is proven. He walks to the bus stop directly outside the parking lot and sits on the empty bench inside the shelter. As if sensing the young man's need to be elsewhere, a bus arrives shortly at his stop, and saves him from the humiliation of being seen wearing his uniform in the middle of the day. Although David could care less about his clothes, and what other people think of them. The young man's main priority is getting home as soon as he can. He walks onto the bus, pays the toll, and searches for a seat. Due to the time of day, the bus is sparsely filled, and he's able to easily find a seat in the back.

The lack of people onboard offers David the prospect of a relatively peaceful ride, but he's unable to enjoy it. Questions about the future bounce back and forth in the young man's mind, begging to be answered, but David is incapable of coming up with a solution to a single one. As a result, his ride is consumed by endless and hopeless questioning. Luckily, his stop grants him a reprieve from the frenzy of inquiry taking place in his mind, and the chance to think of something else. However, what's replacing the young man's inner turmoil is merely a marginal improvement.

As the bus comes within a few feet of his stop, David pulls the cord above his seat. The action is accompanied by the ring of a bell, which signals to the driver that he's ready to deboard. The bus stops in front of the shelter, and David exits through the back door. As the bus drives away, he intently scans the area, and all the people in it. On a normal day, David would take the bus to work at nine and return around five. To save money, he would typically walk the rest of the way home, but during the darker months of the year, the young man would take a second bus. On occasion, he would splurge if he didn't feel like walking, or if his surroundings made him uneasy, but this generally wasn't an issue. The dealers, drunks, and homeless didn't bother the young man, and he never gave them a reason to.

Their business was their own, and David saw no need to get himself involved in it. Shockingly, the scene today is completely different than normal. The sidewalks are nearly empty, the store fronts unoccupied by their usual loiterers, and the buses breeze by the empty stops without a second thought. Still, David continues to be vigilant in the face of this seemingly tranquil scene, knowing from experience how foolish it would be to let his guard down. He crosses the street at the crosswalk beside the bus stop, but when he reaches the other side, a nearby liquor store catches his eye.

His initial impulse is to continue walking on, but a tempting thought crosses his mind, and leads him to go against his better judgement. So, instead of going straight home, he turns left, and heads to the liquor store. The owner of the establishment greets David as he walks through the door, and he carelessly returns an acknowledgement back. He heads straight to the refrigerated section in the back, where the cases of beer are located. He scans the different brands, but none of them stand out. Though not his first time drinking, the young man has yet to develop a preference when it comes to alcohol, and without any way of knowing which beer tastes best, all of them look equivalently appealing. Although, the taste of the alcohol isn't David's true concern anyway. After a few more minutes of looking, he settles on a case of lager, and takes it to the front.

The owner asks him if he's purchasing anything else, and he answers no. Expecting to be asked for identification, David pulls out his wallet and searches for his ID, but the owner only asks him how he's going to pay. Without missing a beat, David takes out his debit card, and places it on the counter. The man snatches it up and inserts it into the card reader. The purchase is approved, and the machine begins printing a receipt. David and the owner watch the white piece of paper slowly emerge from the card reader, and the second it's finished printing, the latter grabs it and hands it to the former. David takes the receipt and case of beer, and returns outside, heading in the direction of his house.

To his delight, the walk home is quiet and uneventful, and after making it inside, he goes straight upstairs. He places the case of beer on his bedroom floor, kicks off his shoes, and falls onto his bed. He looks at his nightstand, and the silver picture frame sitting on top of it. The picture inside depicts the young man and his mother after a day of playing at the park. He stares at his joyful younger self, and his beloved smiling mother. Memories of the past flood the young man's head, bringing with them a torrent of emotions. The overflow is too much for David to bear, and he turns his attention to the case of beer beside his bed. He grabs one, rips the top off, and guzzles it down.

The pain persists, however, so he grabs another. By the time the effects of the alcohol arise, the young man has gone through the entire case. David spends the rest of the day laughing, and the entire night throwing up and weeping. The next day is spent recovering, and the one afterwards used to reorient himself. Not ready to give up yet, David drags himself out of despair, and looks for a new job. But no matter where he applies, or what he says during his interviews, he's always denied. The given reasons are always the same, not meeting the qualifications of the position, but the young man knows the truth. He knows his arrest is the true reason why they won't hire him. He knows it is a stain that will haunt him for the rest of his life.

Chapter 12

Officer Gonzalez wipes away a loose crumb on the bottom of his lip and crumples his napkin into a ball. He places it into the white paper bag on his lap, and remarks, "You should join too." His partner, Officer Lathom, laughs and says, "I don't know if that's the best idea. I mean what if the Sergeant found out?" Gonzalez smirks and replies, "Half the department are already members. There's not much she can do about it anyway. After all, we're not doing anything illegal." Lathom takes a sip of his coffee and remarks, "I hear ya man, but you know how easy it is to get caught. All it takes is one over sensitive snitch and you're on unpaid leave." All of a sudden, their conversation is interrupted by a dispatcher, who says, "Calling all nearby units. Reports of shots fired on 67th and Peoria." Officer Gonzalez grabs the radio and replies, "Copy, this is Gonzalez and Lathom. We'll head on over." As he places the radio down, his partner says, "And I was just beginning to think it was gonna be a quiet night." Gonzalez sighs and remarks, "Duty calls." The two officers fasten their seat belts, and Gonzalez takes the car out of park. As he slowly inches out of the empty concrete lot, he activates the lights on the car's roof, and turns on the siren. The flashing blue and white lights illuminate the dimly lit area, and the blaring siren alerts everyone close by of their presence. The blue, black, and red car speeds down the street like a bullet, ignoring every stop light in its path.

Signaled by the siren and flashing lights, vehicles quickly move out of the way as the patrol car flies past them. For an amateur, weaving through traffic at such high speeds would be a death sentence, but for the seasoned officers, it's child's play. It takes the police officers nine minutes to reach their destination, and Gonzalez turns the siren off as they come within a yard of the reported street. He slows the car to a crawl, and scans the surrounding area for anything suspicious. However, the sidewalks are empty, and nothing seems out of place to the two officers. They're vigilant nonetheless, and after Gonzalez parks, they carefully exit the car. Lathom looks around and says, "I don't see anything." Due to it being nighttime, much of the street is obscured or difficult to make out, and to get a better view, Officer Gonzalez walks onto the sidewalk. Lathom opens the passenger side door to get a flashlight, but he's interrupted by his partner, who suddenly says, "I think I found something."

Lathom swiftly shuts the door and rushes to the other side of the car. He meets his partner on the sidewalk and asks, "What'd you find?" Gonzalez points at the brick house in front of them, and remarks, "It's open." Lathom looks at the small brown building and notices the front door is open. The two officers draw their guns, and Gonzalez slowly leads them up the stairs. On the porch, they split, with Lathom taking the left side of the door and Gonzalez the right.

The two men look at one another, and the latter whispers, "Ready?" Lathom nods, and Gonzalez enters the house with his gun raised. He takes out his flashlight, and uses it to inspect the dark room. The floor is littered with trash and empty beer bottles. As Gonzalez walks further into the house, Lathom moves to the doorway, and asks, "See anything?" Gonzalez steps over an empty box, and replies, "Just trash." Lathom sighs and catches up to his partner in the front room. The two of them carefully examine the first floor of the house, starting in the bathroom and ending in the kitchen. The house is in such a horrendous state that the two officers have trouble believing anyone could live in it.

Trash is on the floor of every room, and in the kitchen, scraps of food and discarded wrappers are mixed in as well. In the bathroom, cockroaches, and other insects scurry across the moldy tile floor in search of shelter. The filth is too much for the two officers, and they quickly retreat to the front room after finishing their inspection. After getting some fresh air, they re-enter the house, and Gonzalez points his flashlight at the staircase on the right side of the front room. He climbs the stairs, and Lathom follows behind him. They lead the officers to a small hallway with two rooms, and they silently separate to search them. Lathom picks the closer one, and as he enters it, he flicks the light switch.

The ceiling lights weakly turn on, revealing a sea of half opened boxes, and curious, the officer walks through the room and looks through them. He finds a box full of books and pictures, and another with toys and board games. "Jack, come here." Officer Lathom asks, "Why, what's up", and Gonzalez replies, "I think I found our shooter." Lathom hurries into the other room, and mutters,

"Jesus." The two officers stare at the dead body on the bed, and Gonzalez remarks, "Guess we should call it in?" Lathom looks around the messy room and asks, "You find a name?" Gonzalez points at a driver's license on the cluttered dresser next to him and replies, "David Parker." Lathom steps over an empty beer bottle and walks up to the left side of the bed. Immediately, he notices the bullet wound on the side of the man's head, and the large blood stain beside it. Gonzalez goes to the right side of the bed, and picks up a small gun lying on the floor. He shows it to his partner and says, "Found the weapon." Lathom sighs and remarks, "I guess he couldn't take it anymore." Gonzalez places the weapon on the end of the bed, and replies, "I guess not. I'll call it in." He exits and heads back downstairs, leaving his partner alone in the room. Lathom stares at the dead man and lets out a disgusted sigh. He shakes his head, and mutters, "Good riddance."

Little Black Boy

Little black boy, you are loved.
Exalted by one from above.
You wear a crown upon your head.
So pay no mind to what is said
Life is yours to do as you wish.
Never limit yourself to a swish
Even though you will face strife.
Do not think less of your life.
You are greater than you know.
Your skin need not look like snow.

Made in the USA
Columbia, SC
28 January 2024

30526588R00095